Tattoo

Tattoo

by Michelle Rene

AnnorlundaBooks

Dedicated to all the miscreations out there.

Contents

Chapter One: *They*

The motley assortment of beings congregated just below us in the shade of the multilevel garage. Concrete spirals of cars and oil-stained walls towered over the group like a Goliath. Most of the creatures were human, and one was a scraggly poodle dog that danced impatiently about an older woman's feet, wanting desperately to be held. The timid one, now known as Jane, lifted the dog and held it to her chest. The ever so subtle wag of a tail indicated the beast's happiness, and Jane scratched behind one of its ears.

We stood above the company, our presence unknown to those who argued and planned below. Some subconscious force moved me toward my companion as though her presence was a comforting hearth. When I did, her arm brushed mine. I couldn't help but look down and compare our arms side by side. Mine was rough and chiseled. Volcanic ash and scarred flesh. Hers was perfect, a pristine specimen like the rest of her. She was a vision with her mane of red, curly tendrils dancing in the breeze — her ivory skin, her firm and curvaceous body. An angel of a woman contrasted against my brute ugliness.

Those sparkling eyes narrowed as she concentrated on the gathering below. A millennium of knowledge flooded those deep pools of hers. I could get lost in them, but there was a danger there too. One could drown in eyes like that and never see the light of day again.

"Stop it," she said abruptly.

"Stop what?"

"Don't be coy. It doesn't suit you. You are just as beautiful as I. And, after all, what does it matter to ones such as we?"

"It doesn't," I snapped. I hated when she peeked in my head that way.

The long, breezy gown she wore was her favorite. It was truly a part of her like her own hair. We wore no disguises here. No one could see us. We could be ourselves wholly, even if it was not fashionable for this time. I wore my uniform bound about my waist, leaving my skin exposed, pocked and scarred for all to see. The flesh on my torso and neck would remain forever scorched in my natural state, my black skin edging into hard lines of gray and cinder. Many scars covered my body, but the largest, the one that still hurt regularly, ran straight across my abdomen with all the violence of a lightning bolt. I could still smell electricity when I touched it.

"It's beautiful, your scar," she remarked gently. "Things like that are lovely. Reminds you that you are different, unique in all the world."

"It never feels beautiful."

I snorted a little at the musing of a woman who had no scars of her own.

Soon, the collection below us had made a plan and set off on their way, hoping no one would see or hear them. It was dangerous, what those small people had done, what they had decided. Little did they know the two beings on top of the parking garage had heard every sentence they had uttered and all the ones they had not.

"They are going into hiding," I said.

"Yes. A good plan, I think," she replied.

"Shall we help or hinder?"

"I think neither."

I looked at her with an obvious question in my eyes. My face was always serious even in confusion. She almost laughed at the comedy of my expression. As it was, all she did was smile. The feeling of patronizing humor never did sit well with me, not from her. Of course, she used it all the time. Why did I fall prey? Why did I love it so?

"So you believe our intervention here is at an end?" I asked.

"For now, I think so."

"She only has five followers."

"Yes. An insane mother, a youth savant, a protector, an artist, and an atoning man." She counted them off on her delicate fingers.

"Sounds like you've birthed a brand new arcana for the girl. It doesn't seem like enough. The last time there were more."

"The last time was different in a lot of ways," she said with a smile.

We watched from our perch as the group of misfits walked away from us, all crowded around the fragile girl in order to protect her. She held the dog, since it was one of the only things she herself could protect. None of them knew exactly why they were drawn to the girl, feeling the need to protect her. Perhaps they never would.

The corners of my mouth pulled downward in frustration. I could feel it in the tension around my jaw. She stood at ease, but I knew she could feel the troubled waves of energy radiating around my cindered body like heat bubbling beneath rock. Nearby was a bench bolted to the rooftop where a parking spot should have been. It looked like some fool's misguided attempt to make this asphalt flat a haven for leisure. I left the angel and sat there, agitated by the events.

"Five seems too sparse," I said with a huff of hot air. "I do not approve."

"Five is plenty. They are all capable," she replied over her shoulder.

"She is so fragile," I said.

"She is stronger than you give her credit. Give her time. She's barely gotten room to adjust to this place."

Dissatisfaction and worry fought for control on my face. They both felt like tension, so it was a pointless battle. She glided over to me and placed one delicate, white hand on my rough shoulder. I could almost feel a breeze from the folds of her gown when she did that. Always she remained a soothing and confident wave to my anxiety, even if she sometimes caused it.

"The last time was different. I like this gathering. They will protect her," she mused.

A light screech broke the silence of the afternoon, and I flinched imperceptibly for a second before realizing what it was. I gazed over at her, but she didn't seem to notice my moment of panic. Old memories of screeching birds, burnt flesh, and terrible pain flashed in front of me. The scars on my body stung.

A lovely white owl soared downward to meet us. She lifted one arm and the creature landed gracefully, clenching its talons into her arm's flesh. The owl was used to this perch, and she neither winced nor bled under its grip. Instead the two nuzzled one another with an intimacy I envied. For an instant, I wondered what it might be like to be that close with another being, even a bird.

"You can borrow her if you want to know," she said, answering my thought.

The owl screeched disapprovingly.

"I think not," I replied. "I've had enough birds in my life."

"This one won't hurt you. She's a lamb of a thing."

When I saw the owl, my shoulders relaxed a little. Despite the label of bird, I had to admit there was something about owls that was naturally soothing. Perhaps their faces, round and delicately white. Such a calm way about them even when they murdered their prey. Nothing hard or vile. Not like the birds I had known. The ones who tore flesh and ripped out my soul every day again and again. The owl screeched, flew away, and brought my mind back to the present. I sighed heavily under the weight of what we'd done.

"Your father will not be happy about this," I said rubbing at my largest scar.

"I doubt he'll lift his head up long enough to care. Retirement has made him fat and lazy. He rarely concerns himself with the happenings of mortals any longer."

"He might lift that heavy head of his for this one."

I tried not to show the sadness in my voice. Something in it trailed back to a time long ago, before the humans, before the fighting, when her father and I were friends and allies. For a moment, I reached back through time and space to recall an era before the scars. My vision went dark and cloudy with remembrance.

"You don't worry about retribution, do you?" she asked, bemused. "Father may have sent tortures your way, but it was so long ago. Surely you are not still walking around with that in your chest. It was a lifetime ago."

The lovely woman turned to me, a half smile gracing her mouth. It was the look she wore when asking a difficult question but trying to do so with a note of humor to lessen the sting. I knew every trick of hers, every piece of guile. Still, they always worked. There was nothing that escaped her crystal gaze.

"Some fears never truly go away," I grumbled.

"Father has no power anymore. You know that. He no longer cares about the ways of lower creatures. They do not believe as they once did. We are mere novelties to them now. Stories told in the history books. Fancies of ancient bones."

She sat down next to me, moving the air in such a way I could catch her scent. Parchment and flowers and sandalwood and even a little death. How easily blood and books mixed inside her. Such a dichotomy.

From seemingly nowhere, she retrieved a tobacco cigarette. It was hand rolled and expertly at that. So strange to see a frivolous human thing in her fingers. She cocked her eyebrows toward me and motioned to the cigarette.

"I could use a light. Would you mind, darling?"

Darling? Oh, she did know how to turn me even when I was bitter. I offered one finger toward her, making the tip of it burn. She pressed the cigarette to it and inhaled until she puffed out smoke. By the time she pulled away, the tip glowed.

"Thank you," she said, blowing out a long, smoky breath.

The acrid smell of burning tobacco became a third passenger in our conversation.

"Why pick up such a worthless habit?" I asked.

"Why not? Occasionally the mortals come up with some good ideas. Too bad they are on the verge of wiping this one out. It's entirely pleasant. Besides, it's not like I have to worry about lung cancer," she said with a little chuckle.

She picked a bit of leaf off her lip and flicked it away. Despite the hot sun, she leaned in to me and curled up against my shoulder like a small child. Her mane fell down the length of my arm. Against my better judgment, I shut my eyes and enjoyed the sensation.

"What are you thinking about?" she asked. "I can hear your mind whirring."

"I'm nervous about the girl," I lied. Well, it wasn't a complete lie. I was nervous about the girl, but my mind bounced around for so many other reasons as well. What we had done, this little project into which she had roped me, tread on some dangerous ground.

"I like this gathering of protectors. I told you she will be all right."

"I don't know."

"Do you doubt me?" She raised her head so she could look at me. "Have I ever steered us wrong? Do you not love me?"

"I do love you," I professed, even though I wished it weren't true.

"Why would you think that?" she asked. "Why would you not want to love me? It's written in your mind. All over your mind, in fact."

She appeared hurt. Genuinely.

"I'm sorry," I said, latching onto a shred of hope that this was true. "I am only afraid you don't love me in return."

Another long billow of smoke eased from her mouth as she regarded me. Her face was stoic, unmoving in a way I could not read. If only I could see into her mind the way she saw into mine, perhaps the playing field would be level. All my questioning would cease. The idea she might be manipulating me to play her games poked at me incessantly. I was no fool, but I loved her like one.

"Don't be silly," she said. "I convinced Father to release you all those eons ago. Of course I love you."

Something in me relaxed as another thing tightened.

When she stood, she took a final drag of her cigarette. Without so much as a warning, she stubbed out the butt on my cinder-like shoulder. The black ashes left a spattered smudge. I couldn't deny the hurt.

"Why did you do that?" I asked.

"Oh come now. It isn't as if you felt it," she said.

She moved back to the edge and looked down. When I rose, the old uncertainty about her affection returned, but I pushed it down in the hope she wouldn't read it.

Gazing at the street below, we saw nothing of the party. The reporter who had been rendered unconscious was waking, dazed and looking up into a small crowd gathering around her. She pointed a shaky finger in the direction into which the small group had run off. Several people armed with recording devices ran toward the parking garage where we had last seen the girl and her protectors.

Instinct pushed me forward to intercept. A delicate hand stopped my progress.

"Don't. They are already away," she said.

"How do you know?"

"I have faith."

"That is a funny thing to say. Faith is what these people are lacking. Look at them below. Gathered to witness a spectacle. They want a show at the expense of something beautiful," I said with contempt.

"I understand your feelings, but they haven't all gone that way. Just the ones you see below. Our girl has already attracted five good souls, has she not? It's not a population, but it's a start. Give them enough time, and the world will right itself again. At least, they will get it pointed in the right direction. Our little project will not have been in vain."

I considered this for a moment. The lower beings led futile lives and held brittle beliefs that could be remade a thousand different ways. So many quibbled over the trivial and murdered over less, blind to the divinity they carried.

There was the other side. Kindness and love. Forgiveness. Passions that filled the air with music and the walls with stories. It was the reason I'd trespassed so long ago. I saw the potential of their souls and helped them when it was forbidden. My punishment was to be chained to a mountain and tortured by birds for all time, until she came to rescue me.

However, I never could shake mortals as others had. Love had won the day, despite the pain. I never could forsake the lot. No matter what my torment, I always held a tender place for them. Why was that?

"Because dear old friend," she answered my thought with a smile. "They may have forgotten about us, but we haven't forgotten them."

Chapter Two: *Natali*

———◦———

The day the girl came to general lockup started out on a weird note. There had already been three fights, one I had to single-handedly dismantle, and the lunch bell hadn't even rung yet. The inmates were restless and fidgety, as if it was a full moon or something, like animals before a big storm.

Officer Beine called me over to help her, wide-eyed shock plastered on her freckled face. Something had spooked her, something significant.

"What is it?" I whispered.

"Can you take this one to cell five twelve?"

"Sure. Why?"

"I-I don't want to."

I gaped at Officer Beine. She wasn't a big woman like me, but I had never known her to freak out over an inmate. This woman had once stabbed a shot of adrenaline in the chest of an overdosing inmate without hesitation. Now, her eyes darted back and forth a little, as though looking for movement in the noonday shadows.

"Okay?"

"She's in holding. Thanks."

Keeping your cool is essential in prison. The inmates are afraid mostly, but fear backs a person in a corner of their mind that makes them dangerous. So, as I rounded the corner that led to the only holding cell currently occupied, I steeled myself for anything.

The kid sat on the one bench the tiny cell provided. That's how I first labeled her, a kid. She was small, fragile-looking, like a life-sized porcelain doll. The difference was this doll looked back up at me and blinked her huge, brown eyes. I thought of a cow or something as seemingly innocent. When the realization hit me, it hit me hard. The thing that was wrong with this picture, the thing that made Officer Beine afraid.

The girl was completely unmarked.

Not one tattoo covered her pale body. She was completely unwritten. Everyone since the big judgment day had their life tattooed on their body. *Everyone* did. Not only that, but she was bald. There wasn't a strand of hair on her head save some thin, brown eyebrows. Not a mark, not a hair, not a past, not a future. I held onto my breath, for it threatened to catch.

"Inmate Sparrow?"

"Yes?"

"This way, please."

She batted her long cow eyelashes at me and stood, collecting the bedroll and pillow that had been provided for her earlier. This kid was so spindly, so delicate. Once the fear subsided, all I wanted to do was put my arm around her in comfort. She looked so afraid. More so than any other inmates I had escorted.

"We are going to cell five twelve."

"Okay," she replied.

Inmate Sparrow followed me in silence, and silence was what followed her. Everywhere we walked, people stopped whatever they were doing and stared. A group in the back of the common room ceased their card game to gawk. Two inmates ended their telephone conversations to watch us in our silent procession. Some muttered inaudible curses; some whispered hastily to one another. There was an overall unease vibrating through every hall we passed.

The kid sort of tucked in on herself, trying to act as invisible as she could. I wondered if she could sense the change in the air her presence caused. It was a dumb thought. Of course she could. Who wouldn't?

Inmate Sparrow. I had to make sure I didn't get it twisted. She was an inmate, nothing more or less. Inmate Sparrow. Not kid. I couldn't imagine what a little thing like her had done to get slapped in prison, but no matter what, I had to think of her as a prisoner.

We reached cell five twelve to find the other three residents sitting on their bunks chatting. I knew them, they weren't the worst bunch, not the best either, but they had a vacancy, and they were all white. Admin normally kept like with like. It was a notion that seemed silly to me, but statistics showed that in an environment such as prison, the races adapted to better with their own kind, so to speak.

The thing was, the second the women looked up at the kid, they all froze. Wide-eyed and mouths agape, the inmates shrank a little on their bunks while staring at the two of us. The air got thicker. The kid and I couldn't help but tense. The air-conditioner kicked on and nearly had us all jumping out of our skin from the noise of it.

I recognized these three enough to be shocked by their reaction. They were not particularly violent. Sure, there were tiffs here and there, and they showed their muscle when it was necessary, but I would have never pegged them for the killing kind. However, the looks they were giving us made me wonder. Was it fear? Was it hatred? Both, I thought. This kid was something new, something unexplained. She was the embodiment of things they didn't know. Her life was a mystery, and her mystery could be deadly. In prison, inmates thrived on the status quo. Anything more was a threat.

Of course, no one would try anything with Officer Cruz nearby, but what was going to happen to this girl when she wasn't around? What was going to happen when the lights went out?

"This is your new cellmate, Inmate Sparrow."

The women turned into frightened animals, tensing as the kid entered the cell. The looks on their faces should have been accompanied with snarls, but there was no noise except the sounds of women talking a few cells away.

An old memory crept into my skull – the one with the little white girl in school. I was always a big child for my age and a proud one. The kids sometimes called me Mexican when I was really Honduran. That earned them a beating. Not a bully-type beating because I wasn't a bully. My intentions were not to be mean but to defend my heritage and me. I was the good guy, the one with the flitty cape and everything.

Then, one day, there was this girl who said I looked like the maid who cleaned her house. She was small and rarely talked to anyone, a little stuck-up thing with a pasty complexion. She always wore scarfs and snooty blouses that frilled around her neck, like a model in a magazine. In a rage, I slapped her face at recess and ripped off her turtleneck blouse for all to see.

She cried in a corner while everyone laughed, but there was no mistaking what I read tattooed on her neck, what everyone read. Her father hurt her bad. He did it a lot, and only her housekeeper, a Honduran woman named Jaime, protected her. But Jaime wasn't there all the time. Jaime had to go home at night. I read that in the words on her skin and in her tearful eyes.

When she said I looked like the maid who cleaned her house, it was meant as a compliment. She loved Jaime.

Suddenly, I wasn't the heroine or the good guy. The world shifted. That sparkly cape broke off of my shoulders and flew away from me and the evilness I caused. My clothes turned all black, and I could see how easy it was to lose. It was so easy to be wrong, to be evil when you thought no matter what, you were always right.

I helped her up, apologized, and walked her to the nurse's office. After school, I wept into my pillow, disgusted with how ugly I had become. The harsh truth, the dark reality was that the line between good and evil was a blurry one, and people were rarely one or the other.

This time though, Inmate Sparrow was the fragile kid in front of me, and I was the Honduran housekeeper keeping her safe as long as I could. Eventually, I would have to leave her here. Eventually, I would have to go home and leave her with...

"What was that, Inmate Sparrow?"

My tone was sharp, so sharp the kid jumped before she turned around to look up at me. The other women did the same. It was my go to voice for ending conflicts.

"I-I didn't say anything," she whispered.

"You want a mark for that kind of talk?"

Inmate Sparrow looked at me, puzzled.

The other inmates mirrored her expression.

"N-n-no, Ma'am."

"That's Officer Cruz to you, Inmate."

My voice was getting louder. A few people started appearing in the hallway, trying to glimpse a hopeful spectacle. I knew how far I could make my voice reach. There was a technique to make it bounce off the walls. It was far enough.

"I'm sorry, Officer Cruz."

"That's it! You're coming with me, Inmate Sparrow. I will not have back talk like that in my prison. You are going to solitary."

I grabbed the kid by the arm as I tucked her bedroll under the other arm. With a quick yanking movement, I launched her and myself into the hallway. The idea was to go for spectacle, not pain. I didn't want to hurt the kid, just make a good scene. She stared at me in astonishment.

We made our way to the next block over, where the solitary cells were kept. A few were filled, but the place was never completely vacant. Officers rarely liked putting inmates in the Hole. It was much better to earn the inmates' respect and let them want to behave for you than to always threaten with punishment. This time, I knew it was the only way.

"Officer Cruz, I'm so sorry for –"

"Hold on, kid."

We reached an empty cell, and I guided her inside. I hated that it smelled vaguely like urine in one corner. Without a word, I took her bedroll and laid it out on the steel cot for her. Normally, we didn't allow the normal bedding in solitary. The inmates got thinner mattresses and blankets instead. It was supposed to be a punishment. This one wasn't here for that, so I set up her nicer bed and filled out a permit slip from the pad in my pocket. I, Officer Cruz, gave permission for Inmate Sparrow to retain her bedroll. She watched me in silence as I slipped the paper under the pillow.

"There we go. No one should bother you about this now."

"I don't understand."

I turned my gaze up at her. That thin face of hers was still clenched in confused fear.

"They won't take your bedroll away with this permit slip."

"No, I mean, what's going on?"

"This is solitary."

"I understand that."

"Good, and you saw what those other girls were like?"

She nodded. A flash of recollection flitted across her face.

"So, you are in here now. You'll be safe here."

There was one slow nod before the water welled up in her eyes. In a flash, she ran to me and threw her arms around my neck in a sincere embrace. Despite my training and my better judgment, I returned her embrace. She was so small under my arms. It was almost as if she was a sparrow, as her name suggested. When we released each other, the usual embarrassment I would've felt over hugging a near stranger never came nor did she look anything but grateful.

"What's your name, kid? The one people call you."

"Jane. My name is Jane, Officer Cruz."

"All right Jane, get some rest. I'll be nearby if you need me."

And I was. Normally, gen pop was up my alley. There was always something going on. The little cliques and tribes milled about, working through their own schedules. Occasionally, there were fights or drama. In gen pop, the hallways throbbed with dozens of moving bodies, moving minds. The air was dense with the humidity of everyone breathing so close to one another. It wasn't peaceful detail, which is why I liked it. It was best to keep busy to pass the time.

Working the Hole wasn't fun, but it was plenty exciting, just not how I preferred. It was quiet most of the time in that eerie way. Then, without warning, someone would hurt themselves or spit at you when you delivered their meal. The little bit of respect I earned from the gen pop girls didn't apply in the Hole, even if they were the same inmates as before. Nobody was the same in there. Not you or the inmates.

The day after I locked Jane away, I put in a request for shifts in solitary. I got them no questions asked because no one really wanted those shifts anyway. It was a lonely, thankless business, but some little part of me, the part that still wanted to wear that flitty cape, knew I had to be near Jane. She needed me.

I didn't know what she was in here for, no one seemed to, even her. Normally, if there was any doubt of an inmate's crime, one day on shower detail cleared everything up right away. There was no getting away with anything when your life was tattooed on your body. A few had been put away because of body tampering. They had had enough money to erase their crime and have some shiny, new memory inserted instead. Some jobs were good; some were hacked. Mostly, if you ended up in here, the job was a hacked one. If it was a really good one, you probably would've never gotten caught in the first place.

Perhaps that was the unsettling thing about Jane. Her body was hacked, but there was no sign that anyone had ever touched her. Even the best tattoo artists couldn't erase *everything*. Not only that, but nothing was ever added. She stayed blank. Jane walked about having a life with experiences and yet, nothing got recorded. No one knew what to do with her. How could you know where you stood with a person like that?

Solitary is by its nature a lonely place. It is a punishment. Since we are social beings, being alone for so long a time is torture after a while. I didn't want my decision to keep Jane safe here to be a punishment too, so every day, I went into her cell to talk to her.

"Where are you from?"

"I'm not sure."

"Who are your parents? Do they know you are here?"

"I had parents, sort of. I mean, I remember parents that I didn't actually have."

I could feel my brow furrowing. Sometimes, the kid made little to no sense. "What do you mean?"

"I mean I didn't have any memory of anything, until a tattoo artist gave me a life. I could remember the life she gave me so vividly. She said she had to kill off my parents because it would be the most believable thing. It hurt so much to lose them."

"You had a tattoo artist give you a new life?" I asked, disbelieving.

My little Jane had consorted with a criminal like a tattoo artist? Was that the reason she was in here?

"Yes, but it didn't take. The next day I woke up with no tattoos at all. I did remember the life she made for me, though. It wasn't as real feeling as it was before. More like a memory of a life I watched someone else have. I'm not good at explaining."

"How did you end up here?"

"I was walking on the street. It was so crowded for a while; I thought I might be safe. Then, some men started following me. Their eyes were bad – I don't know how to describe it – dark in places that should be light. Parts of their insides must have been ugly to make them look like that."

"Skin dealers," I muttered.

"They followed me until the streets weren't so crowded. There were fewer and fewer people to hide me and keep me safe. I kept turning down corners, hoping to find more people, but I ended up alone. There was only vacant buildings and barbed wire on the roofs. The men got closer, and blocked off all of the ways I could have gone to get away. Someone...a woman...helped me. We ran until we found a police car. I was so grateful, but when the police man got a better look at me, he asked me to go to the station with him."

"And that's why you're here?"

"I guess so. Why is everyone so afraid of me?"

I was going to answer her. My mouth was open and everything, ready to explain the primitive nature of people. Why we were afraid of something new and different, even if it's beautiful. She was so lovely...

The beeping of my watch alerted me that someone wanted to talk with me. With one finger to my mouth, I asked the inmate to be silent. I pulled back my sleeve and touched the answer button on the call screen.

"Yes?"

"Officer Cruz, Inmate 427RJ361 has a visitor."

I looked up at the girl in front of me. The white stripe of fabric across her lapel read 427RJ361, a number assigned to her a week into her confinement. Jane looked suddenly afraid.

"She's in solitary. Solitary doesn't get visitors."

"They do when it's their lawyer."

I touched the mute button and glanced over at Jane again.

"You have a lawyer?"

She shrugged.

"All right, buzz the lawyer through. I'll meet him at the gate."

I left her there, promising I'd be back.

He was not as I expected. In fact, I knew this one. He was the sort-of famous kind, but not the cheesy commercials you see on TV at three in the morning when insomnia hits sort-of-famous lawyer. I had read about him on news feeds.

Most lawyers who came to a place like this fit into two categories. There were the do-gooders and the moochers. The do-gooders didn't have much money, and they were generally trying to help out the common person. They were few and stretched thin, to be sure. Their suits were threadbare and their eyes tired. Normally, these were the type who was assigned a case. Mostly, these were all losing cases.

The moochers chased the prison buses. They wore cheap, flashy suits, spinning whatever yarn about being able to overthrow faulty forensics. They normally represented the hacked-job skin cases, people who had tried to cover up their misdeeds and failed...miserably.

This one, though, he was a new one. Lawyers such as him rarely visited prisons like mine. If a man like that was representing you, you normally had to have the money for him, and if you had that, you had the money to pay for one of those nice suites in the corporate-owned prison on the other side of town. Doing time there was like going to a restrictive resort for a while. Massages, gourmet meals, and the like.

This guy, in his suit that probably cost my rent, smiled at me as if I were a living person. I felt myself glaring a little and tried to cover my skepticism better. Charm never was a strong point of mine. Too much lying and concealing.

"Officer Cruz."

"Yes."

"Elliot Mansel. I'm here for Inmate 427RJ361, Jane Sparrow."

"Yeah, I heard."

He looked at me square, sizing me up. I didn't move. I could take this guy if I needed too. I didn't imagine he was much under that suit.

"You going to take me to her?"

"What are your intentions?" I wasn't giving this guy an inch, not one.

He laughed with in a smirking way. "My intentions? What are you, her father?"

"I'm whatever I have to be."

He faced me, eye to eye. I only had to look up at him a little, but what I lacked in height, I made up for in strength and know-how. He was soft in all the places I was hard.

"My intentions, Officer Cruz, are to be her lawyer. The order came from on high, Judge Taylor himself. Now, do you plan to escort me to her, or should I call for someone else?"

I knew of Judge Taylor – everyone did. The order really must have been from on high to bring a suave guy like this around. He held up under scrutiny; that I gave the man. Trust still did not flourish between us, but I relaxed my guard a little and nodded for him to follow.

The solitary block was quieter than usual, and I wondered whether the other inmates were listening hard, as if they could sense something bigger coming this way. When I opened the door to Jane's cell, I watched the lawyer closely for a reaction. He flinched, obviously unnerved by her, the way most seemed to be. He hadn't met her before. That wasn't what I wanted to see, though. What I looked for was what came next. His face would either be wrought with the kind of fear I had seen in the other inmates' eyes or the kind of fear in mine.

The air felt electric while I waited for his personal verdict.

His eyes softened into a knowing, a wondering, and then I recognized it. He was afraid but not because she was a kind of different that was terrifying and wrong. That face of his reflected a deep need to protect her from others, and the fear of what they might do to such a fragile creature. I instantly liked him more, and left them alone to discuss her case.

Mr. Elliot Mansel came often during the following weeks to talk with Jane in private. She liked him and told me he was going to help her. The lawyer's eyes said something else to me. Sure, he put on a good face for Jane, but the second he left her cell he seemed to sink into himself. I felt a little sorry for him. It looked as if the weight of every person in Dallas rested on his shoulders. Every time I saw him, he smelled more and more like bourbon.

Once, he looked up at me, wiped his brow with a kerchief from his lapel, and spoke. "You always here, Officer Cruz? Don't you have a home or something? I never come here without your lovely face staring me down."

It was a compliment and put-down in the same sentence. One of those back-handed ones. For anyone else, I would've been offended, but this guy? After weeks of watching him operate, I figured this was a respectful icebreaker or sorts.

"No one much likes solitary detail. I don't mind it."

"You watch this one close, don't you?"

I shrugged. "She needs someone to."

"Well, you and I both agree on that one."

He stared at me with this unreadable expression I could only judge to be kind of grateful. Not the entirety of grateful, but related to it. Grateful's cousin maybe. The man looked as if he'd been through the wash and hung up on the line. Elliot Mansel bid me a half-hearted farewell then took his leave.

Weeks passed, and every time I saw Mr. Mansel, he seemed a little more beleaguered. I wanted to ask Jane what was going on, but the news told me enough. Someone had got wind that she was here and what she was. Images of her frightened face appeared all over the TV. People began showing up at the gates of the prison and outside city hall. Some were the religious types who called her an angel. Others were the religious types who called her a devil. Still others picketed the judges and the courts, saying she had rights and to set her free. Being unmarked was no crime. Some held signs up saying we should test her genetics and find a cure. Bring anonymity back to the masses. None of these were the right kind of people to be around Jane. All of them wanted to exploit her for one reason or another.

I went home from a double shift one day, exhausted and feeling every day of my years. I had been forced to drive through a thick crowd of bodies at the prison gate. Most held signs calling Jane all manner of things. There were posters with her picture on it, some with painted wings behind her and some with bullet holes in her head. The dichotomy was horrifying. One man held a sign with a verse from the bible I knew.

Behold a pale horse: and his name that sat on him was Death, and Hell followed with him.

My Jane was that pale horse? Not in a million years. She was everything frail and true left in the world. The temptation to run over the man was intense, but I pressed on, glaring at him as I made my way through the crowd. Still, my foot itched to press the pedal.

When I got home, the TV was worse. The news of Jane's upcoming trial consumed everyone's programing. I couldn't even escape it at home. Throngs of women wearing white gowns camped out in front of city hall, their heads shaved smooth. They called themselves Jane's Angels. A strange Asian woman was interviewed, claiming to be Jane's mother. She was treated with all the respect her story allowed. Even though the woman was old enough to play the part, Jane was definitely not Asian, and nothing about her looked like this woman at all. The newscaster catered to the obviously crazy woman but eventually panned away to someone else. The thing that struck me was the woman's conviction. She was serious. She really believed Jane was hers. There didn't seem to be any motive other than that of a mother.

My thoughts about that stalled as I caught movement in the background of the news piece. There a large crowd around the newscaster, but away in the fringes, just on the edge of the crowd was a face I knew. Well, I didn't know him specifically, but I knew the markings, and I knew the look.

He was bald but wore a sweatshirt, the hooded part over his head. Those eyes on him were the eyes of the vulture, the scavenger, the hyena. They were the eyes of the villains my Abuela would tell us about in old stories. Across his forehead were the words that almost always labeled his kind for everyone to see.

GREED

"Flesh dealer."

The word sent a chill of fear down my spine. After I said it, I picked up the phone and asked my manager if I could start pulling triple shifts in solitary.

It was a long day right before Jane's trial was to begin. I had been up all night and was scheduled to work all day. Officer Marks was supposed to relieve me then, so I could sleep, but I demanded to be on Jane's security detail the next morning on the way to the trial. As per usual, I opened the door of solitary to escort the lawyer. Most things were becoming habits and involuntary motions for me. The world moved around me the way it did with the sleep deprived, like a boring play I couldn't help but participate in even though I had died years ago. What snapped me out of it was when he grabbed my shoulder.

"Officer Cruz, can I have a word with you?"

I was taken aback. The man looked just as haggard as I did, but in his eyes sat an intensity that told me to go along with it to see what was bothering him so much. I nodded, and we made our way out into the little rectangle of yard the solitary inmates were allowed to use once a week for exercise.

"What's going on?"

"She's not going to win."

"What?"

"There is nothing I can do. The cards are stacked against her. Higher-ups don't want her free. They want her gone, one way or another. Her presence brings up a lot of questions. This is an impossible case to win."

My mouth hung open. Words refused to form.

"I need your help," he said, quieter than before. "I need you to help me get her out of here. We can't let her make it to trial."

"I'm sorry. What are you asking me?"

"I'm asking you to help me make sure Jane is gone from here before her trial. If she goes to trial, there's no way she will win."

"Are you asking me to help you break out your client from prison?"

A shadow passed over his face, as if he suddenly realized he might be betting on the wrong horse. With a deep breath, he placed his bet anyway.

"Yes. That's exactly what I'm asking you to do."

My glower lasted a long while. He twitched under my scrutiny. For the first time, I noticed his tie was lopsided, and the circles under his eyes were about as deep as mine. The long nights worrying about Jane hadn't been mine alone. I thought about her and the flitty cape she put on my shoulders.

"All right, Mr. Mansel. What did you have in mind?"

He smiled despite how exhausted he looked, and laid out our plan.

———◦———

The next day was the trial. I buzzed open Jane's cell door exactly at eight in the morning. She stood looking very thin in the orange jumpsuit that fit her the way a tent might fit a flagpole. When her eyes met mine, they were relieved. She ran to me and hugged me around the neck.

"I'm so glad you're the one taking me."

I hugged her back. There was a slight sour smell in the air, as if she'd been sick.

"Nervous?" I asked.

"Yes. My stomach won't settle. I'm so afraid."

"Don't worry. I'm here, and Mr. Mansel is waiting outside for us."

She brightened, which said a world of compliments for the lawyer.

I cuffed her hands together in front of her and chained them around her waist as loosely as I could. A silly precaution for someone like Jane, but it was part of the rules, and appearances needed to be considered for the time being. We walked to the front in anticipatory silence.

When I opened the doors, a cavalcade of voices flowed in as well. A din swelled around us, threatening to swallow us whole. Jane cringed next to me. I thought she might faint at any minute, but Mr. Mansel was next to us in a flash. He threaded one arm through the crook of her elbow and steadied her on her feet. I walked a little ahead, with one hand positioned on my gun. My hackles were up and my senses peaked.

We had been forced to erect a temporary fence along the path from the front gate to the parking lot where the shuttles were. All types of people crowded against it, pressing themselves into the chain link to get a better look. They shouted praises, questions, and curses at us as we made our way along the protected pathway.

"Jane! Jane! Is that your real name?"

"Do you worship God?"

"What sort of abomination are you?"

"The Devil! The Devil lives in her skin!"

"Praise be to Jane!"

She tried to shrink into the lawyer, and he covered her as much as he could with his jacket.

"My client has no comment other than she is completely innocent."

"Jane! Jane! Jane!"

"Angel Jane, save us from ourselves!"

"Kill her now while we still can!"

I flipped the latch that held my gun in place in my holster, ready to draw it if needed. When we reached the edge of the cacophony, I looked around for the shuttle bus. It wasn't there. The receiving area was deserted. Instead, a tinted black Town Car pulled up to the opening in the fence. The windows were so dark I couldn't make out the driver. Mansel hadn't told me about a Town Car. I turned to the lawyer with a questioning glance as they caught up with me.

"This is our ride," he said. "Trust me."

We opened the back door and piled into the peculiar chariot. The slam of the car door was followed by a quick spinning of tires and the car's acceleration. A thick black screen partition separated us and the driver, a blindness that made me nervous. When the car left the prison's gravel drive and turned onto the nearest road, the wheels spun and squealed a bit underneath us again. Terror filled me. I braced my whole body for action. The lawyer just pounded his fist against the partition and yelled.

"Damn it, Dakota! I said drive casual!"

The black partition rolled down with that automatic hum, and a woman peered back at us with an excited smile. Her short, green hair stood out in a strange pattern from underneath a chauffeur's hat. One side was shaved.

"Sorry about that. I haven't driven a car like this in years."

"Dakota!" Jane practically squealed when she saw the green-haired woman. Her eyes lit up, and she made to try to hug her but didn't get very far in the crowded back seat.

I felt the tiniest pang of jealousy somewhere inside my chest.

"Hey, kid. Don't worry. We are getting you outta here."

"Give me your hands," I told Jane.

She did so, and I unlocked her cuffs. Then I unwound the chain from around her waist while the lawyer dug a parcel from under the car seat. He produced a set of clothing, and Jane changed inside the car with us.

"You mean, we aren't going to trial?" asked Jane.

"No way. You weren't going to make it through a trial. We have to get you out of here."

"Where are we going?"

"Dakota is driving like we are going to the courthouse to not draw suspicion, but we are going to switch out cars. The parking garage downtown is near a lot of other parking garages. There's a van in one of them with clothes and provisions. You, me, and Dakota are going to run away somewhere. Camp or something. Get out of town. We have to hide you away from people."

I looked at him, flummoxed. He had told me about the other car and about the other driver, but not beyond that. The story was to say they overpowered me and stole my gun, but where would they go? He never told me. Why had I not thought to ask?

"You are leaving with her?"

The lawyer gave me a level look. "What would your solution be? To keep her in solitary?"

"No, but..."

"We don't have time to discuss it. Hiding Jane is the primary goal."

Dakota took a right turn a little rough. Buildings seemed to surround us suddenly. A gauntlet of skyscrapers, like glass mountains, rose so high around us it was hard to see the summit from the ground. We were approaching downtown.

"Dakota, take it easy," he barked at her.

"I'm nervous," she snapped.

"Look, Cruz, you just tell them we pulled a gun on you and give us a good fifteen-minute head start. That's all we need, and you can go back to your life."

"And you are going to just abandon your life here to go into hiding with Jane?"

It was a real question, and he took it seriously. That heavy look he'd been carrying fell over his eyes again, but he didn't answer immediately. When he did, it was a whisper. "Yes."

I turned to the driver and nodded at her. "You too? You ready to give up everything to hide this girl?"

"Yes," she said, looking back at us in the reflection of the rear-view mirror.

The word *pride* bobbed up and down on her forehead as she did. I looked back at Elliot Mansel, Mr. Big Shot Attorney.

"Why?"

He sighed deeply, glancing at Jane before meeting my gaze again. "Because it's the best damn thing I've ever done in my miserable life."

A smile threatened to invade my face. I knew exactly what he meant.

"Okay. Me too then," I said.

"What? Why?" he asked.

"Because I have the fucking gun. That's why."

Everyone fell silent, and Jane giggled beneath her hands.

"But camping is a no go, chief. We can't hide in the woods forever. We need another plan," I said.

"Says the woman with the gun?"

"Says the woman who really hates freakin' spiders and shitting in the woods and desires a practical future. Tents are not a practical future."

"Any suggestions, then?" he asked, more than a little annoyed.

"No, not really..."

An oppressive silence infected the luxury car. No one seemed to know a good way to say this plan was doomed.

"Four Points," said Dakota from the driver seat.

She had pulled into a parking spot inside a garage and slammed the car into park. We were in the shade. The only sound was the muffled rumble of cars driving on other levels. When she turned around to meet our faces, she was smiling like a lunatic.

"Four Points?"

"Yes, Four Points."

"Start making sense, Dakota," said the lawyer.

"My family in Louisiana. They own a fish camp down on Four Points. I went fishing there all the time in the summer. It's huge, with like five bedrooms. No one goes out there anymore. It's in the middle of nowhere. We could live away from people, in hiding. The closest town is Dulac. It's tiny Cajun country. We'd be invisible."

Our party of four contemplated that for a moment. Well, I contemplated it, and hoped the others were leaning toward the direction that didn't include spiders.

"Not a bad idea," said the lawyer. "And if it doesn't work, we'll work from there."

"Good. Now, let's get out of here. Where is the van?" I asked.

"One block over. Let's go."

We extricated ourselves from the Town Car and made our way to the stairwell. The goal was to get to the ground floor undetected by the throngs of people camped only a block away in front of the courthouse. The only sounds we made were our footsteps on the stairs and the panting breath of the lawyer as we ran down four flights.

By the time we hit the ground floor, it was already too late. A bright light nearly blinded all of us as the constant prattle of a reporter pelted our ears. I shielded my eyes from the light and saw the plucky blond anchor from the Channel Eight newsroom blocking our path with a handheld recording device in her left hand. The device had a bright light on it, and she was using it to illuminate Jane.

"Miss Sparrow, what are you doing here? Are you not supposed to be going to the courthouse right now for your trial? Does this mean you are pleading innocent? Guilty? Are you escaping custody, Miss Sparrow?"

Jane starred into the light, terrified and confused. The white light seemed to make her skin glow. Stunned and silent, Jane shone like an angel or an alien or a ghost. She looked over to me for help.

My hand was on my gun, and I was ready to pull it on this woman. Another second, and perhaps the scenario would've played out that way. I might have had a chance to forever stain my soul with her blood. That all might have happened, except a small Asian woman and a tall black boy shoved the reporter from behind and knocked her down. The boy grabbed the portable recorder while the woman pulled a pocket canister of bear mace out and blasted the reporter in the eyes with it.

We all backed away. The smell of the mace filled the air, and we covered our faces when the stinging hit our eyes.

The reporter writhed and wriggled in pain, but the woman just kept the spray going until there wasn't any more left. Then, she flung the empty canister and hit the reporter on the head with it. In that instant, the only sound in the air was the yipping of a little poodle dog dancing around the woman's feet.

This would have been hilarious under any other circumstances. Right then, it was all about survival. I looked at the kid who was checking out the recorder.

"Was it a live feed?" I asked him.

"No," he said. "No, looks like she was just recording. I'll erase the video."

He did so and threw the machine on the ground. A few hard stomps and the device was in pieces. We were breathed a collective sigh of relief. The news anchor got to her hands and knees, vomited her breakfast on the pavement, and struggled to crawl away from us. Her eyes were swollen shut under a stunned, red face. It wouldn't do to have her crawl away, asking for help, so I rendered her unconscious with one good knock to the head. Guilt filled my gut when I saw her go down. She would probably have a concussion, but there was no time. The din of the crowd nearby reassured me she wouldn't be lying here long. Someone would surely find her soon, and they would find us too if we didn't move.

When I turned around, Jane was hugging the young, black guy. His hair was cut short and he wore scrubs like a nurse or doctor might. Jane's face was full of happiness.

She obviously knew him from somewhere and was glad to see him. Next came the woman. She began to cry as she collapsed into an embrace with Jane. Relief poured from her with every sob into Jane's shoulder. The poodle thing pranced around her feet, wanting desperately to be held.

"My darling, my darling. My little Janie. Mama's missed you so."

Something clicked in my brain. The Asian woman looked exactly like the woman I had seen on the TV. She was the one claiming Jane was her daughter. The others seemed just as skeptical and confused as I was.

"This is your mother?" asked the lawyer.

Over the woman's shoulder, Jane shook her head ever so slightly. She hugged the woman tighter, despite the negative answer.

"Of course she is my daughter," said the woman, pulling away from Jane. "I've been searching for her for years. Finally, you've come home, darling. I found your young man too. He was waiting at the courthouse, trying to see you."

"Thank you both so much," said Jane.

"Well, this is a touching reunion, but we've got to go," said Dakota, looking around anxiously. "This won't be the only plucky reporter trying to get the story."

"She's right. Let's go," said Elliot.

"We are coming too," said the boy.

"Yes. We go where Janie goes," said the woman.

"What is this? A fucking field trip?" asked Elliot.

They both looked silently resolute. The din a few blocks away got suddenly louder, and we all flinched, ready to bolt at any minute. Time was running out.

"Oh fine. I don't have time for this. Follow me before we all get caught," said Elliot.

These strangers were ready to follow Mansel as long as he was headed where Jane was going. I could understand this thinking for only one reason. I was ready to do the same thing. Something about this girl, this fragile little thing, inspired the truest form of people. For all of us, it was the call to protect. We were her knights in shining armor, her super heroes in flitty capes. There was no point arguing the fact. This motley band of strangers was bound together because for better or for worse; we were the good guys.

Chapter Three: *Elliot*

She may or may not have been a hooker. Her dress was high class enough to be a professional woman letting her hair down for the evening, or she could be a rather expensive call girl. The dress was green and slinky, and clung to those perfects breasts of hers for dear life, the way I wanted to. Her ass was narrower than I normal went for, but hey, I wasn't picky.

"Ready for the reveal," she whispered seductively.

"Sure."

I leaned back in my designer chair upholstered with the finest blah-blah fabric from Turkey or Ethiopia or some shit like that. It had been my grandmother's, like most everything I owned. Even the house had been hers. She was a mean old bat, but she had taste. I was sad when she passed, regardless of all the stuff she left me.

With a slow spin befitting a pole dancer, Cindy dropped the translucent wrap she had been wearing along with that green dress. I thought her name was Cindy. It sounded right, but I couldn't think clearly because she was in her bra and panties in front of me. Not much thinking was happening at that point.

The tattoo wound around her body and ended just below her rib cage, telling me either she lied to me about her age, or she had lived a lot of life until that moment. I was on the pretty side of fifty but the ugly side of forty, and my tattoo barely made it past my waist. Surely, she was older than I thought, because I had been no slouch in the living life department.

At first glance, nothing about her life story jumped out at me from the tattooed writing on her bronze skin. She had grown up in Southlake, with a-well-to-do family from the looks of it. Graduated college from SMU. Liked affairs and had two abortions. A few skeletons, but nothing I hadn't seen before. Cindy was a pharma rep, just as she had told me at the bar. I had wondered if it was a lie, but sure enough, she was no hooker. A miniscule wave of relief passed over me, as I was a little cash poor at the moment, despite my inherited designer surroundings.

When she felt her little reveal was at a close, she pointed to me.

"Your turn, stud," she said with a sexy smile.

I stood and collected her in my arms. She was a solid little thing, and I kissed her with all the passion I could muster for a perfect stranger. A whisper of the chardonnay I had bought her at the bar lingered on her breath. I'm sure mine smelled of bourbon.

"Ah baby, let's be rebellious. I'll turn off the lights and be anyone you want me to be."

Believe it or not, this tactic worked most of the time. In a world with no anonymity, where your entire life story was tattooed on your body for all to see, one-night stands were a tricky thing. Plenty of women swooned at the idea of imagining me to be whatever they wanted instead of the reality of what I was. This one, however, was not biting.

Cindy pushed me away and crossed her arms over those nearly perfect breasts of hers. A dissatisfied line made up her once-beautiful mouth. "Not a chance. If you have herpes or something, I want to know."

"I don't have herpes."

"Then you won't mind showing me."

I sighed. There was no recourse left. I would have to oblige her. My only hope was for her have terrible nearsightedness that she was too vain to correct with lenses or surgery. With noticeable reluctance, I removed my shirt and stood before her like a lamb at the altar.

She surveyed me for a few minutes and said nothing. Fleeting hope filled my addled brain. My body was nothing like hers, but I had managed to stave off the stereotypical gut men my age seemed to flaunt. It wasn't tight, but it wasn't flabby. When I heard no objections, I moved forward to try to kiss her again. With one dainty hand of steel, she stopped me.

"And the back. Come on and turn around, cowboy."

My face was aflame just thinking about what was going to happen next. I knew what was coming, but I turned around for her anyway. This lamb was headed for the abattoir, and there was no stopping it. My broad back was exposed to her delicately wondering eyes. It was only a matter of time.

"Oh, you've got to be kidding me," she snapped.

Her barbed words flew across the room and hit just to the left of my spine, where I knew the offending bit of information was etched perfectly. I winced at the invisible pain as I heard her begin to gather her things. She was beyond exasperated with her lost evening, and I was not about to explain or try to stop her.

"You are fucking gross."

She stormed toward the front entrance, exited my opulent digs, and slammed the door.

"I know. I know I am."

The next day, I took a long lunch and went to visit Dakota. When I walked in, she was blessedly alone in her piercing shop in Deep Ellum. A little bell jingled when I opened the door, and Dakota gazed up at me from some art magazine she had been perusing. There was a new tattoo on her since I had seen her last. The word *pride* was written in the maker's perfect script across her forehead.

For a long minute, as we stared at one another, I wondered what she had done to earn that.

"You got a reason for the visit? I'm pretty sure we are paid up, counselor," she said in that plain way she liked to speak.

I had done some legal work for Dakota a few months back. Even though the piercing shop was perfectly legal, her side business was less so. It was this side business that brought me to her. She was good, she was discreet, and I knew she never bought from low-class skin dealers.

"I need some help."

"That I can see."

"You available?"

"Yes. No one normally comes around until the evening time. What's your pleasure, counselor? We are having a special on nipple piercings, buy one get the other half off. No pun intended."

"I'm not looking for that."

"Hmmmm. I never pegged you for a ladder sort of guy, but we do that too."

"Not that either."

"Well then, are we going to dance around all day, or are you going to lay it on me?"

I drew a big breath and let it out. Dakota's eyes widened at my obvious embarrassment. She was going to see it all. Everything I had done to Wendy.

"I need some tattoo work done," I said while trying to focus on her eyes.

"Indeed? You got money?"

"I'm a little cash poor right now."

"I see? And how were you planning on paying me?" she asked.

"If you do this for me discreetly, I will forever be indebted to you," I said.

"How so?"

"Any legal fees or favors you may need are on the house."

"For how long?"

"As long as I'm around to perform them."

Dakota's eyes widened with alarm. For a woman operating an illegal business such hers, the offer was more than tempting. She had her bribes out to correct people, but you never knew when the correct cops were going to get replaced. The wheels were turning in her head. I could see it in her face, and by the fact she didn't tell me to fuck off right off the bat.

"This must be a doozy of a job."

"It's just embarrassing, and I'm ready to be rid of it," I said looking down at the floor.

"Okay. It's a deal. Follow me into the back room," she said as she made her way past the glass cases of jewelry and through an entrance with a thick curtain.

"Said the spider to the fly," I muttered under my breath.

"I heard that."

"Sorry."

The place was a little dark, but clean. She motioned for me to make myself comfortable on a cushioned chair that looked like one of those massage things. There was cradle for my face and everything. It smelled the way an old lady's couch smelled when covered in plastic.

"Take a good swig of this first," she said, handing me a bottle of cloudy, purple liquid.

"What's this?"

"Something to ease you into this."

"I can't get loaded today. Will I be able to work after?"

"Sure. Just eat after we're done."

I threw back the whole bottle, removed my shirt and tie, and relaxed onto the chair. My bare back was exposed to Dakota for her feminine judgment. I heard her move a stool closer, and there was a strange sound too, like a whir of something electrical. Delicate, gloved hands maneuvered their way gently over the globe of my back, revealing my life story.

"So, which things here am I taking away?"

"All the ones that would make a woman not love me," I replied.

She made a ticking noise with her teeth and tongue as she surveyed my landscape.

"That's a tall order, my friend."

I felt her hands danced close to the area just to the left of my spine.

"Had a thing for livestock, did we?" She was suppressing a laugh.

"I grew up in the country and was drunk a lot, okay? Besides, you don't hear me asking you about your newly acquired face tattoo, do you?"

The half-hidden giggle inside her dissipated, and she returned to her scrutiny.

"What's the verdict?" I asked.

"I see three main events here that probably need to go. The obvious one involving...your...country living, the one about your friend, and the one involving Wendy. Sound about right?"

"Yes."

"All right then. The stuff you drank should be numbing you pretty well by now, so I'll go ahead and get started."

"Wait, Dakota."

"What's up?"

"Leave the one about Wendy."

She looked again at my flesh and placed a gentle hand on the part of my back where the Wendy affair resided. I hadn't killed, raped or even married her. I had done something so much worse.

"Are you sure? In my opinion, it's one of the biggest offenders. I mean, you obviously loved her, but you left her in that motel room alone with a bloody mess. It was your fault she got pregnant in the first place."

"I know, but I don't want to forget Wendy, even if it costs me dates. There were good times too. Just the other ones, please," I said while trying to disguise the quiver in my voice. "I just...I just don't want to forget her entirely."

"I could leave some of her. I don't have to take it all," she offered.

"There are some things that shouldn't be forgotten, so you know not to do it ever again."

"Okay. It's your skin, counselor."

When the deed was over, I felt so much better. I couldn't even remember what the stories were that Dakota had removed from my life. Well, I could, but they felt like memories of a movie I once saw as opposed to my memories. That was why she was so good. Most of Dallas and half of Fort Worth went to her for things like that. Whatever she had removed had been replaced with some masterfully woven story of her own making. I didn't feel a loss at all. No gaps, no blank spots, no missing pieces.

I felt lighter somehow, relieved of an ancient burden I could no longer recall. I waltzed back into my office building, whistling. My secretary looked at me with a confused expression. I dug into the complimentary candy dish on her counter and asked how her morning had gone.

"Fine?" she said, as though it were a question.

I pulled out a hard butterscotch candy and grimaced. "Evelyn, can't we get some less shitty candy in here, I mean really? Something with chocolate?"

"You asked me to throw out all the good candy. Said it was too tempting."

"I did! So sorry, but I've just been a total ass lately. Let's go get some better candy. You only live once."

I was perky, and she didn't know how to handle me.

"Mr. Mansel, Judge Taylor is waiting in your office."

"He is? You didn't offer him any of this terrible candy did you?"

"No sir."

She couldn't help but gawk, open-mouthed like a fish at me while I smiled a toothy, idiot grin into those heavily painted eyes of hers.

"Good. Well done, Evelyn. You are so helpful."

I strode down the hallway, greeted a few confused interns, and opened my office door to see a grave-looking Judge Taylor sitting in my chair. He was sucking on what was obviously one of Evelyn's terrible candies. I grinned, thinking what a good liar she was.

"Judge Taylor," I said as I walked in, my hand outstretched in greeting.

"Mr. Mansel," he responded seriously, taking my hand and shaking it.

"What brings you here today, sir? Not Evelyn's terrible candy, I take it."

"No, that's not why I am here. I have an assignment. I'd like to assign it to you."

He never did have much of a sense of humor, but the judge's whiskered face looked more solemn than I last remembered. The silvery white hair was plentiful for a man his age, and he wore it down the sides of his face as mutton chops. Their whiteness stood out starkly against the good judge's dark skin, almost like a caricature of a style rather than the look of a real man. His dark eyes were grave, and I took what was normally the visitor's seat, allowing him to return to my seat behind my desk.

"Do you remember the before time, Mr. Mansel?"

"Please, sir, call me Elliot. We've known each other so long."

"The before time, Elliot. The time before tattoos and the judgment day?"

"No, sir. I'm afraid I was too young to really remember."

"Well, I do. I recall a time when babies were born pure and without their birthdays etching into their scalps. People were unmarked unless they wanted to be. Then, it was a matter of choice to tattoo yourself with some image or saying or something. A girl from my neighborhood had an entire illustration from a book running down her arm. It was beautiful. Back then, the justice system had to work to convict people. There had to be evidence and proof beyond a reasonable doubt. You couldn't just catch the criminal and read their body to see if they had done the deed. Forensic scientists were used to gather evidence and prove guilt through DNA testing and fingerprint analysis as opposed to what they are today—just a bunch of brainy fellows who are relatively good at deciphering if someone's story had been counterfeited or not by a tattoo artist. Can you imagine what it must have been like back then, before God stole our anonymity?"

"I honestly cannot imagine, sir."

"Well, you had better start."

"What do you mean?"

"There is a young woman in custody right now who is completely unmarked."

My eyes felt as wide as dinner plates, and I was sure my mouth fell open. Surely, I had heard him wrong.

"She's...unmarked?"

"That is what I said."

"Is it natural or counterfeit?"

"The boys in forensics say natural."

"How? How is that possible?"

"I don't know, but I went and met with her myself. She hasn't a mark on her. She doesn't know who she is or where she came from. Claims a tattoo artist made a life for her to help her blend in, but it vanished the next day. She won't give up the name of the artist."

I gaped at the old man, waiting for some sort of hint he was joking, but Judge Taylor wasn't the joking type, and his face never faltered.

"Does she remember anything?"

"She seems to remember waking up in the hospital a few days ago. Some people helped her escape, then the tattoo artist, and then a halfway house. A squad car picked her up yesterday on the street running from some sketchy people. She has memories, but none of them are written anywhere on her."

"She's lucky the flesh dealers didn't get to her first."

"True, that's one blessing, but now, Elliot, we come to the crux of the matter. This girl has to be put on trial, and I want you to represent her."

"Trial? We haven't had a trial in years. Since..."

"Since your defense of the Borgie brothers."

"Judge Taylor, that was so long ago..."

"...and you were brilliant."

"Thank you, sir, but what exactly is this girl charged with?"

Judge Taylor lowered his eyes, and I could tell there was shame in there. For some reason he had a soft spot inside his old body for this girl.

"Failure to register."

"What?"

"It's silly, I know, but nothing she does registers on her body. It's like the old days with her, and we are not a society that can handle someone like that any longer. Gone are the days when a person could easily hide their infractions. A girl such as this could be a criminal or a target, and there is no way to register the events in her life. She could do anything, and the governing body of the United States would not know. I'm afraid she is on trial for her anonymity."

"Sir, how on earth can I possibly defend this girl?"

"That is something I hope you can figure out. You are a brilliant lawyer, when you are sober. I believe you could've held your own in the old days. Right now, a young woman needs your help. Please don't leave her waiting."

I didn't.

After a quick straightening of myself in the men's bathroom, I headed directly for county lockup. The guard on duty was an odd duck. All bluster and muscle. However, she had a way about her that read well. A sparkle in her eyes said she had something behind them worth knowing.

When I first saw Jane, her appearance was so shocking I gawked like a bystander at an accident. The bald head with the perfectly unmarked flesh was jarring. I experienced a kick to the chest the second I saw it. But those eyes, those big doe eyes of hers, they told me more than what wasn't written all over her. She was afraid, no, she was terrified sitting in her little cell all alone.

The first interview was more or less small talk—we were becoming acquainted with one another. Jane didn't seem to remember much of anything past a few days previous, and even her name had been invented by some tattoo artist who had tried to help her out. She wouldn't reveal the artist's name, but I had a good inkling who the culprit was. It wasn't just mere coincidence that Dakota suddenly showed up with a fresh forehead tattoo. Dakota was the best in town, and the only one I could imagine who would dare try such a stunt.

I could have interrogated Dakota, but I figured I wouldn't have to. She was my client, after all, and we had all that attorney/client privilege between us. Plus, I guessed it was only a matter of time before she learned what had happened to her little pet project.

Sure enough, the reporters caught wind of Jane's incarceration, and before you knew it, her picture was plastered all over the evening news. You couldn't watch a show or scroll through a newsfeed without seeing it, and I was her lawyer. My name accompanied her photo wherever it went.

The next day, a bedraggled Dakota came bulldozing her way into my office with a new hairdo. She had dyed it green and cut it short, with one side completely shaven. A new coif of bangs hid her unfortunate new label.

"Ms. Dakota. May I help you?"

"You are her lawyer?"

"Please be more specific. I am a lot of people's lawyer."

"Don't play dumb fuck with me, Elliot. You are Jane's lawyer."

"Yes, I am, and you are her mysterious tattoo artist who tried to give her a legitimate past."

Dakota looked as if I had shot her in the chest. Panic swept over her face. "She— She mentioned me?"

"Not by name, so get your hackles down. I guessed as much. But no worries there. No one is looking to prosecute you for something we don't even have proof of. All the tattooing you did is gone," I said, lowering my voice.

"It's all gone? Every bit of it?"

"Yes. There is no proof that you did anything illegal."

"Well, there is if you read my ribcage."

"Then I suggest, as your attorney, to not take your shirt off in public."

Dakota gave me a look that spoke volumes, and the first word of those volumes would have been a proper "fuck you."

"So, what do we do?" she asked.

"What do you mean?"

"To get her out of prison," she said exasperated. "She doesn't belong there."

"I know she doesn't, and you know she doesn't, but do they?"

I pointed to the flat television glass mounted on my wall. The throngs of crazy people camped outside city hall and the courthouse were getting even thicker than the night before. It was a terrifying mixture of crazy zealots, curious onlookers, and violent psychopaths.

"What is she charged with?"

"The crime of being unmarked and thus, unable to live as a contributing member of society. Trumped-up charges that never existed until now, I know, but they are afraid of her. No one knows what to do with a permanently unmarked girl."

"Well, what are you going to do to get her out? What's the angle?"

I sighed. This was the crux of the matter, was it not?

"I don't know yet. I'm trying to think of something."

"I'll testify," she blurted. "I'll tell everyone what I tried to do. It will prove she really doesn't remember anything."

"That won't help our cause. It will only prove that she can't ever be marked, which means we will never be able to re-introduce her into society if we cannot trace her misdeeds. Plus, it will most certainly call attention to your ribcage and put you in jail for a very long time."

Dakota's brow furrowed, and she bit her lip. Tension radiated from her body. It was an emotion I was unaccustomed to seeing in the tattooist. Dakota's nature, or at least the one she showed the world, was that of quiet calm, the pierced Buddha. It's the demeanor you wanted to see in a tattooist or doctor or lawyer. Right then, she was positively leaking anxiety onto my faux Persian rug.

"Why do you care so much?" I asked her abruptly.

She looked at me with stones for eyes—stones that burrowed into my head but had the good grace to say nothing about what they found there.

"Why do you?" she asked.

"Because..."

"Because you met her," she answered for me.

I thought about that for a second. Yes, I had met the girl. Hadn't my whole mission changed after that initial meeting? That sweet, innocent girl and her peculiar ailment had frightened me at first, but after, all I felt was fear *for* her. For what people might do out of their own fear. I pondered my near-immediate instinct to protect her. Not only me but the hard-nosed guard too. That same look danced behind Dakota's eyes as well.

"Yeah. Yeah, I met her."

"Then there's no point explaining our motives here. I want to help."

"I'm not sure how you can. Look, I can't discuss more of the case with you than is in the newspapers. However, if I find a way to utilize you and not put you in jail, I will. Okay?"

She eyed me warily, trying to decide if this was legitimate or just a ruse to get her out of there. Whatever her conclusion was, she didn't share it with me. Dakota merely nodded toward me and left my office with nothing but the memory of her short skirt in her wake. Relieved, I exhaled audibly to no one but myself. My yoga instructor had said it was healthy or something.

During the next weeks, I pored over ancient volumes of law text. Some were older than the judgment day itself. If you had asked me what I was searching for, I couldn't have told you. Anything, I supposed — a precedent, a trial, a freaking haiku. Anything to make the charges against the kid go away. Failure to be marked. In other words, resistance to the status quo. Or in better terms, we are fucking afraid of you because you are anonymous. You have no accountability to the things you do accept to yourself, and we don't know how to handle that.

My one terrible brick wall came from the judicial commandments set in figurative stone after judgment day changed everything.

Every citizen is and always will be marked with their deeds.

A citizen's marks are sacred and inscrutable.

The markings are the basis on which a citizen is judged.

To alter a citizen's markings is illegal and immoral.

How would I possibly get around this? But also, how could a person such as Jane help her situation? It was obvious she never had tattoos. She tried to get a life written for her and it didn't take. Must she suffer for this?

When the prosecuting attorney was assigned, I breathed a little sigh of relief. For weeks I had been dreading this news, hoping it wasn't Rebecca. She and I had a sketchy past in the most sugar coated of scenarios. Robert Willhelm was going to prosecute, and he and I had a good ole boy camaraderie. There was some wiggle room with Willhelm in all this. I called his number and asked him out for a drink.

"I'm afraid I can't, Elliot." Willhelm's voice was standoffish and strained.

The organ inside me that drove my intuition fell deep into my stomach, belly up so to speak. I clenched my teeth. "What? We can't meet at Zepplins for a round and discuss the case? Come on. I'll buy you that drink you like. The one that tastes like sadness."

"Moscato. It doesn't taste like...look...I'm sorry, Elliot, but I just can't."

"Moscato, that's the stuff. Come on, we can't meet at Zepplins for a round and discuss the case? I'll buy you a glass of Mosc-sadness or whatever."

"Really, I can't."

He was serious. No joking in there at all. I began to tense throughout my shoulders.

"Gloves off, Robert. What's going on here? I mean, I know it's high profile, but..."

"Look, Elliot, I'm really sorry they put you up to this one. It was a real shitty thing of Taylor to do. Maybe he didn't know the score, and that's why he asked you. I don't know. Either way, just shut off the switch and look the other way."

"Shut off the switch? What are you telling me here?"

"I'm saying don't care about this one. You won't win it."

He wasn't blustering. There was no room in his tone for it. This was straight truth, and it frightened us both. Still, I had to try.

"Well, you're talking awfully cocky. I mean, Taylor will be presiding over the case, and he's got a soft spot—"

"Taylor's not the judge anymore," he said.

"What? Since when?"

"Since the capital got wind of this. They appointed someone else. Listen man, I'm telling you. It won't matter what you say or do. This girl is going to prison for the rest of her life, and there's no way to stop it. You didn't hear this from me, but the powers that be are making sure of this one. I'm sorry you're the one on the hook. Really."

My jaw was slack. Somewhere in the hallway, I smelled the tangy scent of disinfectant. I looked at my watch and judged that I was one of the only people still working in the building except for the cleaning crew. I tried to say more to Robert, but my mouth was all dry. The words he fed me had been salty and wouldn't wash down right.

He hung up with me after a hasty farewell. I mouthed something back at him, but he was already gone. The idea that the whole thing was doomed filled me like a specter. The ghost of the inevitability of it all haunted everything I did. I was the walking doomed, moving about my life knowing exactly when the other shoe would drop and how and why. What more was there to do?

The day before the trial, I went to visit Jane in solitary. Well, I didn't so much as my ghost did. I was wrecked. Sleep hadn't really been a friend of mine in a few weeks. Life passed around me as if I was watching it on TV. If I said something funny out of habit, I almost always laughed because it was like watching someone else say it.

Officer Cruz looked just as bedraggled as I did. For some reason, that tired expression in those nearly black eyes of hers snapped something loose. It was a kinship of sorts. Like those knowing stones in Dakota's eyes—an epiphany that I wasn't alone in this. Something radical and wonderful filled my brain. I knew it was insane, like something you might see in a movie, but it just had to work. This was going to be the only way to save Jane. We had to take matters into our own hands. The system was going to put an innocent girl away for life, so we would have to get away from the system. We would have to go off the grid. Not only that, but we would need help. Kindred spirit type of help.

I grabbed the guard by her shoulder, causing her to flinch out of her own reverie.

"Officer Cruz, can I have a word with you?"

Chapter Four: *Irene*

For ten years they told me my baby girl was dead. Ten whole years, but I knew better. No one knew my Janie the way I knew her. She was smart, my girl. More than smart, my Janie was brilliant, and not just because I liked to brag. Well, I did like to brag about her, but even the principal of her school told me how exceedingly smart she was when he came to the funeral. I told him I would tell Janie he said so when she came home, and he looked at me that way people do nowadays.

My girl first vanished from our home ten years ago without a trace. She had been playing in the backyard of our little house in Carrollton when a storm rolled in. It was one of those pop-up thunderstorms, the kind we get in the summer, and when I opened the back door to tell Janie to come inside, she wasn't there. Not even a hairband blowing in the wind or a sock left behind. Janie had just vanished. Clouds towered above me in that threatening way thunderheads did. The air vibrated electric. I could smell it on the wind. Something had happened. There was a gap in the world where my Janie should have been, filled with only emptiness of everyday life.

I looked everywhere. The terror, the utter and complete hopeless, immobilizing horror that consumes you when you can't find your child is something every mother knows. They are by your side one second and then they aren't. It's like having a little piece of your soul walking around on the outside of your body where anyone can hurt it. When it's lost, there is no comfort. None.

We looked for Janie for months, and nothing came up. Rescue workers, policemen, volunteers, everyone seemed to huddle around our little hole in the world and try to help us fill it. I kept opening the door to my house, expecting to see her just walk up, twigs and dirt in her hair from getting lost in the wilderness behind our neighborhood. Is wasn't much of a forest really, only by Texas standards, but it was enough to get lost in. She would be so hungry she'd eat a dozen cookies from the freezer before telling me her tale of survival. Then, I'd hug her and say I never gave up hope. That never happened.

One year passed, and my husband wanted a funeral. The authorities had given up on a cold trail with no leads. A grief counselor had suggested a funeral would give us some closure.

"Closure? On what?" I had told him. "Our daughter's coming home."

We had the stupid funeral anyway and filled the small coffin with mementos and photographs. Her friends brought little things they wanted to give her. It was nice, but I took some of the trinkets Janie would have wanted and held onto them for when she came back. I told her friends as much, and they cried. Those tear-filled faces were dutifully shuffled away from me by their parents. Poor kids. They were only nine or ten. Janie's age. They didn't seem to understand she was coming back.

My husband lost faith. That's the best way to describe it. Such weakness some men have. I suppose women can have it too, but it's so much more rare among mothers. When you're a mother, you just don't give up on your kid...ever. I knew my Janie. She was far too smart to just be gone forever. There was no way she'd let someone take her, and if they did, they'd have one big battle on their hands. My girl was strong and strong willed. She had inherited that from me.

My girl was alive. She was hiding out somewhere, waiting for the perfect time to work her way back to me. Janie might have gotten lost, but she would come home. Heaven and Earth couldn't keep us apart. I knew that. She knew that. Mothers and daughters know these things.

After a while, my husband asked for a divorce. It was fine with me. Who would want to be married to such a specimen? Who gives up on your only daughter like that? Weak. That was the only word to describe such a person. Less than a person, really. He was a worm—a weak worm.

The part I didn't like was moving away from the house. I had no particular attachment to it except that it was where Janie had last known me to be. How would she find me in this new place? When she returned, she would find a different family in her home. That would simply be awful. I wanted to stay where my Janie could find me.

In the end, my choice was taken away from me. My husband hired people who all worked together. I knew because they all had the same uniform with little logos on it. They packed up my things, and told me I was to go live with them in a big house near downtown, but I didn't want to go. Besides, they hadn't boxed up any of Janie's things. I needed to have those items with me for the day she came back. Janie would want them.

Everything got blurry the way it does when you can't stop crying. Eventually, the people said I could take one box of Janie's things with me. That was all the leeway I needed. I grabbed the largest box in the house because they hadn't specified the size I could take, and I packed it with all her most important possessions. Almost everything fit, and I took pride in my ingenuity. I was a smart cookie, like my Janie.

When they took me away, my worm husband hugged me goodbye. He was sobbing and apologizing, but I wouldn't look at him. One didn't suffer themselves to look upon worms. After my things were packed into a van, the people in the uniforms separated me from the worm. His tears had wet the lapel of my shirt. I looked down at it and then at him with nothing but scorn.

"You cry like a person, but you are no person."

That's when the people took me away to the big building downtown. Overall, it wasn't a terrible place to live. The air-conditioner was not of the best quality, and the air smelled musty during those few weeks in Texas when you didn't need the cold or the heat turned on, but it was clean all around, and they let me open my window when I liked. The other residents were odd. Some were genuinely crazy. Some were just sad. I had my own room overlooking the street, so that was nice. Everyone on my floor was allowed to wear his or her own clothes, so that was nice too. I heard the people on some of the other floors didn't have as much freedom. Rumors said they didn't even have windows.

A few times a week, we met in group therapy. That's what they called it anyway. If you asked me, it was a reason for a bunch of people to get together and whine. Molly, the red-headed manic girl, mourned the loss of something different every time, and each occasion it was catastrophic. Whether it was a feather, a bow, or her grandmother, the emotion was the same. Ted wore eyeliner and never talked. He just moped all the time. Karlie the junkie was into stealing, and she used group therapy as an excuse to return everyone's stolen items. It was all a game to get attention.

Each of us endured the fake smiles of the counselor and the uncomfortable chairs we were given. It was a practice in patience and posture. Often I counted the little cracks on the walls near the pill counter. Foundation in Dallas was hell on walls and ceilings. Once, a big split in a doorway opened up. One of the orderlies had put a Band-Aid on it as a joke, but when the crack yawned wide enough for the Band-Aid to fall off, it stopped being funny. We were that crack. We all just kept breaking, and no quantity of Band-Aids would cover it up.

Whenever anyone asked me anything, I just said I was grateful for what I had and what I knew. I had the knowledge my daughter would come back some day. The idea once had been that I knew she would come home to me, but this place wasn't home. So, the thought morphed into a different one. Janie would come find me here, and we'd run away together. The thing was, she was a little girl, and I didn't even know where I was anymore. How was she going to find me?

I stopped wanting to eat anything for a while. The people in the uniforms tried to bring me different food, food I had once said I liked, but none of it tasted especially good to me. Noodles were bland and slithered around in my mouth like flavorless ribbons. They reminded me of worms, and then I couldn't eat anymore at all. For the first time since she left, I started to doubt that my clever daughter would find me.

Some group in different uniforms liked to bring in therapy animals once a month. They were mainly dogs, and when they came, Claudette in the room three doors over from me always shut herself in her room with her cat. Sylvester hated the dogs. Normally, I sided with the black-and-white tomcat, but one day, they brought this white poodle dog to us. I was sitting alone in a chair closest to the television, when this ugly thing waddled up to me. I hadn't been eating much, so the whole room looked a bit odd, and my head felt too heavy for my neck. Everything sort of reverberated around my eyes. When I looked over and saw the little dog, I couldn't help but smile. It was the ugliest thing I had ever seen: his white curlicue fur and those tear-stained eyes. Could something be so ugly it was cute?

"Come here, Ugly Dog."

He wagged his tail and leaped into my lap, plopping down without hesitation. I could feel the warmth of his body. I could feel the little rhythm of his heartbeat through his chest onto my thigh. That beating told me a story. That little ugly thing told me not to give up.

The therapy people eventually gave him to me to keep because he was getting old, and I ate as long as he was in my lap. He became my dog, a constant companion and helper. He was my thing to love while we waited for her. I made a collar for him in crafting class that had his name stitched into it.

UGLY DOG

That's what we did for a while, Ugly Dog and me. We lived there in that weird place. We ate and waited for Janie. We went to group, to hear those people whine, and waited for Janie. We took our medicine and waited for Janie.

It happened in such an odd way. The moment she came back was like a moment out of a movie or something. Ugly Dog and I were in our room. Nurse Martin had just left. I had asked her if I could open my window. There was a metal grating on the other side of the glass, so nothing could possibly get in or out. As if I would ever jump out. That was what crazy people did. Besides, the day wasn't sweltering for once, and I wanted to smell the fresh air. Nurse Martin said it was okay. It was in the opening of the window that I first saw her.

A girl, about the age my Janie would have been, was wandering the streets just below me. She was skinny and wearing a hooded sweatshirt, too hot for the time of year. That's the part that made me look closer. My Janie always was cold, even in the summer. Her hands were ice all the time. As I opened the window, Ugly Dog yipped. The sound made her look up at us, and that's when I saw who it was.

My Janie!

It was she. My daughter was looking for me. I just knew she was. Janie was older, her skin was pale, and she was thin all over. Her eyes, those big doe eyes of hers, were different in so many ways but hers truly. It was my Janie. My baby girl had come home.

I ran out of the door and made for the elevator, Ugly Dog hot on my heels. When I got to the bottom floor, the front clerk asked for my ID bracelet before I could leave. We had a system at the house. All those who could go outside wore a green bracelet. We were deemed low risk. The others, blue, red, and yellow all had restrictions. I wore a green bracelet, so the man behind the counter let me and Ugly Dog through.

"Be back by curfew, Mrs. Chen," he shouted after me.

I waved him off and hurried down the street to where I last saw Janie. When I found the part of the street directly under my window, there was no one. I scanned the area. No Janie in sight. I almost wept right there, but no. That would be something the worm did. Not me. I would look for her.

Ugly Dog and I ran a block here, a block there. Cars roared past us. One or two honked when we crossed the street before the light came on. It took us twenty minutes of sprinting and panting and dodging crosswalks before we found her. She was standing alone at the corner of two streets. There was no one around her, but she looked terrified. A silent horror face was slapped across her features.

We ran to her, Ugly Dog and I. As I got closer, I could see a car full of men creeping up toward her. Down the other street, a group of bad boys were closing in. Everyone knew those sorts of boys. You saw them on the news. Blood always followed them. Some of them had the bad tattoos on their foreheads. The ones that said the word 'greed.' She was in bad trouble if those boys were after her. My vision tunneled, so she was all I could see. My daughter was in trouble, and I wouldn't leave her.

Ugly dog and I crossed the street and closed the gap between us before the bad ones could get to her. My first thought was to wrap my arms around her. I did, frightening my poor Janie. She jumped underneath my embrace.

"Oh Janie! I'm here now. Mommy's here. I've got you."

I hugged her. Danger or no, this was my baby. A mother's arms ache to hug her children, and mine had been aching for ten long years. She felt warm and alive in my grasp. I was so happy in that moment. Ugly Dog danced around us, yipping like a crazy.

Somewhere in our rapture, I remembered the danger. I pulled away from her astonished face to see the bad boys only yards away. Ugly Dog and I had surprised them, but I wasn't sure for how long. We had to get her away from them.

"You leave us alone. This is my daughter! I will kill you."

My threat fell on the ears of the evil. They didn't care. Strange, terrible smirks crossed their faces. One started talking to the other.

"You think we can get anything for the old bat?"

"Na, probably not much other than what she'd sell for dog meat."

Ugly Dog growled. It wasn't a ferocious sound, more like a blender rumbling on a low setting. I grabbed Janie's hand and pulled her away from the boys and down a side street that would be hard for the car to follow. Ugly Dog ran right along with us, barking up a storm. I pulled the little metal whistle from around my neck with my free hand and started blowing it with everything I had. The people with the uniforms gave it to us in case we were in trouble. Boy, was I ever in trouble.

I figured between Ugly Dog's barking and my rape whistle, someone would hear us. We ran through several back alleys and side streets before we found other people. Janie and I were breathing ragged and thankful when we turned a corner and saw a small crowd. Plus, there was a cop car. It was parked next to a coffee joint, and the cops looked up when they heard the commotion. We were in front of the patrol car in seconds. Ugly Dog danced around my feet, barking like a triumphant hero. The bad boys had disappeared back into the shadows somewhere. Safety helped me think clearly once again.

"Officer, we were being followed," I said, out of breath. "I've been looking for my daughter here, and these bad boys started chasing us."

"Your daughter?"

The officer looked at me in an appraising way then at Janie, obviously searching for a resemblance. He appeared skeptical.

"I know I don't look old enough to be her mother, but..."

"Wait a second. Miss, remove your hood, if you please."

He was talking to Janie, and she seemed afraid.

"Is she under arrest?" I asked in her defense.

"No, but..."

The cop removed her hood and we all gasped. There, where my Janie's beautiful black hair used to be was a shaved bald head. Not only that, but she didn't have a mark on her, not one tattoo proving who she was. All of her life, her entire life, was gone from her skin, as if it had never happened.

"Miss, are you all right?" asked the other cop in shock.

"Yes, I think so," said Janie.

"You have no tattoos."

"I know. They went away."

"They went away? I see."

"Do you know your name?"

"Jane," she said with a tiny, unsure voice.

Something in that voice, in that declaration of self, snapped me out of my trance.

"Jane. See, I told you. My daughter, Janie. She is my daughter. She needs to come with me now."

I grabbed her hand again and tried to pull her away, but the cops stopped me.

"Is this your mother?" they asked.

I looked her in the eyes, and for the first time, I saw her looking at me. She was searching my face for something. I couldn't tell what she was searching for. Janie shouldn't have to search. She should just know me.

"Miss? Is that your mother?"

With the tiniest shake of her head, she whispered, "No."

In that instant, my heart fell into my gut. Even my vocal cords slipped down somewhere dismal inside of me. All of that, the past ten years, and my daughter didn't even know me. I tried to speak and couldn't find my voice. Darkness engulfed my vision as things began to tunnel. All I could do was look at her with all the hurt I was feeling. All of it welled into my eyes like liquid torment. She must have seen it. Who couldn't?

"I'm so sorry. I just don't remember you. I don't remember anything."

"B-but. I'm your mother. I've been wait-waiting for you."

I didn't feel the cop search me. Numbness seemed to dominate my system. He could have slit my throat, and I wouldn't have cared. Somewhere in space and time he lifted my wrist and read my wristband.

"Says here she's a patient at Caring Touch Psychiatric Center. How did you get out, Mrs. Chen?"

"I-I-I have a green bracelet. Green bracelets get to leave."

The lips I owned were tingly. My eyes couldn't leave hers. It just wasn't possible. They were the same but different. Bigger and a different color than I remembered, but then again, we changed as we matured. It was the bit inside that looked like my daughter. No, not just looked like. Was. This *was* my daughter. No doubt existed in this universe.

"Okay, I see. Hughes, take Mrs. Chen and her dog back to the center. I think Miss Jane should come with me. It isn't safe in this part of town."

He put her in his patrol car and I watched, paralyzed by the whole experience.

"Janie?"

We locked each other in an unbreakable gaze until the car sped her away from me. During that time, her eyes told me volumes. Volumes of apologies. Volumes of confusion. Volumes of sorrow.

I went back to the center without a fuss because I knew the truth. I finally knew the reason why my daughter had been gone so long. For so long, I had pondered what could possibly have kept her away. Now, it was so transparent, I couldn't believe the answer. Amnesia. She hadn't come home because she didn't know where home was. She didn't know who she was. All of her life had been erased from her skin somehow, and that's how she became lost. The loss of her knowing love was almost more than I could bear.

There was no use fighting the cops. They had guns and big laws. What did I have? An ugly dog and a rape whistle. I knew where she was, though, and we would be a family again. I told anyone and everyone who would listen to my story.

Once word got out on the news, I tracked down news people and gave interviews about my missing daughter and how the police were keeping me from her. She had no memory, and they were keeping us apart. What right had they to keep a mother from her lost daughter?

Everything got big and inflated, like a balloon about to burst. People lost their minds about Jane, thinking she was all sorts of things. Angel, demon, an object of ridicule, a thing of praise, everything except what she really was, which was a scared girl who needed her mother. Well, she was an angel, but she was my angel.

When the story got too big, people stopped listening to me. That's when I knew I had to find her and get her away from all those scared and confused people who could cause a lot of damage. Not to mention, those bad boys were still out there, still wanting to hurt my Jane.

I sold my little wedding band at a pawnshop and bought some bear mace and a second hand dress. The pawn lady didn't mind about my green bracelet. She even held the things in the back room for me because I couldn't bring them back to the house without them getting taken. Pawn lady was a mother too. We understood things, we mothers.

The morning of Jane's trial, I went to pawn lady's shop. I changed into the dress in her back room and pocketed the mace. Ugly Dog and I walked five blocks to the courthouse, where we waited among the throngs of crazy, scared people. I was resolute. I was determined. So was Ugly Dog. We would save her or die trying.

It was stifling to be around so many people. The place was an odd mix of cement buildings, car exhaust, and the grass lawn where most of us stood. Asphalt and humidity was a combination that could make anyone crazy. I found no friendly faces in the crowd.

It was then that a young black man moved next to us. His demeanor was soft, if not nervous. His eyes darted around, not finding purchase anywhere he liked. I could feel warmth coming from him. It was like cocoa, like kindness.

"You, young man."

He turned his gaze downward at me.

"You know my Janie?"

All of the oddity and nervousness of his face vanished as he smiled. It was a good-boy smile.

"Yes, ma'am. I met her in a hospital. I was hoping to see her again."

"I'm her mother."

His features turned curious, not skeptical like everyone else did when I said that. Just curious and polite.

"You want to help me help her?"

"Yes. I definitely do."

"You're a good boy. Stay close with us."

Just then, there was a strange noise off to our left, some kind of commotion that most of the people around us didn't notice. Ugly Dog did, and with a loud alarm of barking, he ran toward the ruckus. I grabbed the boy's hand; my other hand was on the bear mace in my pocket. He jumped a little at first, but he grabbed me back. Together, we chased Ugly Dog through a side alley and away from the crazies.

Chapter Five: *Dakota*

———————◦——————

These days I'm considered a criminal. Back before the Big Day, tattoo artists were...well, artists. It was a profession that was out in the open and paid for their artistry. The jobs could be as simple as a bumblebee on someone's ankle or as complex as a memorial scene that covered their entire body. I supposed if someone wanted something like that today, I could technically deliver what they wanted. No one would, though. No one does anymore because every bit of skin that is marred is a piece of their life taken away.

Let's just say Judgment Day wasn't as advertised when it happened. It was before my time, but I read the old texts that predicted seas as blood and the dead walking the Earth. None of that stuff happened. The event was far subtler than anyone expected. We all were tattooed now, from the day we were born until the day we died; our story was written in the beautiful hand of our Maker all over our bodies.

Every major event of our life was etched in perfect script all across us. Even as our skin aged and sagged, the words read just as true as the first day they were scrawled. It seemed like a little thing at first to have your life written across you, but soon the message hits home. Judgment Day was really the end of anonymity. No longer could criminals hide their crimes. If a body washed ashore, the murderer's identity was plainly etched on their skin. When a girl cried rape, not only was the story etched on her skin forever but on her rapist's as well. A policeman's job transformed from collecting evidence to learning to read the nearly extinct art of cursive handwriting.

These days, nothing could be forgotten. Sure, if you went to grab a coffee, nothing about such a mundane thing would appear on your skin. However, if you wanted to forget how embarrassing your one-night stand was or lie to a boyfriend about it, you couldn't. Everything was known, and everything was in the open. Not to mention that your memories no longer faded or glossed over with the silky nostalgia of time. Every person remembered everything etched on their skin with unwavering clarity. That was a wonderful thing if you were reminiscing about your honeymoon in Belize, but what if all you wanted to do was forget that awful person who broke your heart? Sorry, time didn't heal those wounds anymore, and that's where I came in. That's where the Maker and I disagreed.

I spent my young life learning to copy the Maker's handwriting, and I was good. I was damn good. People came to me in tears, begging for relief. They couldn't bear to remember this or that anymore, and I helped them. I expertly removed the strip of skin with the unwanted memory, fixed in a new strip of clean skin, and rewrote that part of their life. When I was finished, the skin looked untouched and they didn't remember whatever it was that I had cut away. This was what a tattoo artist did these days, and it was, of course, illegal.

I may be a criminal, but I'm a clean criminal. I don't cover up crimes, and I don't buy clean skin off flesh dealers. Those people are scum and murder for their stock. All my stuff comes from donors who are prepped and paid. Besides, the cops know me and know to leave me alone. I run a legit business, and the mayor herself was a friend of mine. I helped to wipe away a sad miscarriage for her, and she repaid me with protection.

My legit business was one of piercing and body jewelry. Dakota's Jewel was the name of it, and I lived in a pretty spacious loft above my place. The front counters offered all the latest styles of cheap China bangles that the college girls liked. The back ones had some nicer things and some wooden tribal pieces from Africa that interested the aficionados. We did decent business, but the tattooing was really where the money came from.

It was a Sunday night when the girl walked through my door. I had sent Robert, the pierced kid who worked for me, home early for the evening because Sundays were always so slow. Sunday had become a holier day again, and few ventured out to this part of the city then. I was going to close shop up early when a ghost moved in and rang the little bell above my door.

"We're closing up," I said automatically as I turned around.

The look of the girl stopped me where I stood. She was slight and trembled a little on her feet the way a new fawn might. She was covered from head to toe in hospital scrub pants and a hooded sweatshirt pulled close over her head. Big brown eyes stared at me from under the hood, like a deer lost in a concrete jungle. Her sneakers were a few sizes too big on her feet.

I tensed. "What's your business?"

"Business?" she squeaked.

"What's your game, girl?"

"I d-d-don't have a game."

"No one wears a sweatshirt in Dallas in July unless they are hiding something. Now, out with it."

My muscles were braced to reach for the gun I kept behind the counter. I almost flinched when she reached into her pocket and pulled out a folded piece of paper. With quivering fingers, she held it out to me.

"Nancy...she gave me your name and address...said you would help me."

I relaxed a little and walked to her. The paper was on Baylor's stationery. Nancy was a nurse I knew there, one of many. They sent me the really sad cases, the ones who commit suicide if they don't forget. My face softened looking at the girl in front of me. I wondered what catastrophe had happened to her.

"All right kid, how old are you?"

"I don't know."

I furrowed my eyebrows at her. "Don't play with me, kid."

Tears started welling up in her eyes, and before I knew what was happening, the girl had thrown the hood off her head. There, before me, was a completely bald, completely unmarred, and completely inkless head.

I gaped at her for only a second before I came to my senses. "Oh shit."

Grabbing her hood, I threw it back over her head and rushed her through the curtains to the back room where I did the tattoos and piercings. I ordered her to stay put while I ran back into the store and flipped the sign to *closed*. Within a few minutes, I had shut down the whole store to look dark and unavailable. All I could do was hope nobody had seen her enter.

The room she was in had a heavy curtain and no windows, so it would've been hard to see whether anyone was inside. When I returned to her, she was looking around frantically. I couldn't help but stare at her.

"You're Dakota?"

"Yes," I said. "Nancy told you to come to me?"

"She said you'd help."

"What's your name?"

"I-I don't know that either."

I took a deep breath and let it out slowly, trying to force calm into my joints.

"Do you remember anything?"

She shook her head timidly. "I woke up in the hospital and Nancy...she gave me clothes and...Toby..."

The girl started to cry as she hugged herself. I crossed the gap between us and hugged her. I couldn't help it. The instinct just took over my body. She was like a little bird in my arms as she trembled.

"What's happening? Why don't I look like everybody else?"

"I don't know."

"Can you help me?"

"I can try. Go on now, strip down and let's see what we are dealing with."

She seemed hesitant at first but did as I requested. Under the hoodie she wore a small set of teal scrubs Nancy had probably stolen for her. I gasped a little when she removed those. Before me stood the completely nude and perfectly, serenely unmarked body of a young woman. Not one bit of ink stained her skin. She turned around to face me with the small breasts and a face of a teenager on the cusp of womanhood. I put her at about seventeen, maybe eighteen years old from the look of her. Her skin was so new. Babies' skin wasn't this clean.

I brought the girl a warm blanket from my sofa, and she curled into it as she sat on a nearby chair. There were some orange sodas in my fridge, and I retrieved a cold one and popped the top. She took it and sipped the thing slowly at first as if she had never held a soda before. Once she got a taste for it, she started gulping down the orange liquid as if it would vanish if she didn't.

"Whoa, whoa, easy there," I said coaxing the bottle from her face. "There's more in the back. Don't gulp or you'll hurt your stomach."

"I'm sorry. What is this stuff? It's wonderful."

She took another big swig of the soda.

"It's just orange soda. You've never had orange soda before?"

She shook her head no, and I sat down on the sofa across from her.

"Let's back up here. What do you remember?"

The girl took a deep breath and let it out like a jagged knife.

"I woke in a hospital. I looked around, and everyone was written all over but me. Doctors were making notes and talking in hushed whispers about me. I couldn't hear what they were saying, but I know it was about me. Then, they left for the night and Nancy, she's really nice, she came to me and said I had better get out of there. There was this boy too. He was sweet. He helped me. They said I was in danger, and handed me this paper with your address. She said, 'Find Dakota, she'll help.' Then I came here."

"That's all you remember? That's all you know?"

Tears welled up in her eyes, and she started to cry again. "Yes," she squeaked.

I hugged her as she shook under my arms. My mind grasped at what to do for this girl. She must have had a life at some point. Things had to have happened, had to have been written on this girl at one time, but now, she was alone and frightened, with no history. Not to mention she had a whole body of perfectly pristine skin that any flesh dealer would kill her to possess. A whole body with no history, and no one looking for her.

I pulled away, as her tears began to ease, and held her shoulders. I gazed her into her large brown eyes as she stared back at me. A glimmer of hope flashed in them.

"Listen, you have no life, so we will make you a new one."

"What?"

"We can't have you walking around like this. Flesh dealers will pick you up in no time, and that will be the end of you."

She gasped.

"I will write you a life, a new life, and no one will know the difference. Everything is going to be fine."

My words held a confidence I did not possess. They came from my lips on their own accord, and damn did they sound convincing. The girl wiped her wet face with the blanket. She seemed to believe in me.

"But...but I have no money."

"That's all right. You can pay me in skin."

She shrank into the chair, suddenly uncomfortable.

"Listen, this is what I do. I cut out bad memories and fix in new skin to write better ones. People pay me this way all the time if they don't have money. I always need new skin to use, but I never take it unless the person is willing. If you are willing to pay, I will write you a new life."

"Will it...will it hurt?"

"No. I make my own elixir here. Takes the pain right out of everything, and it tastes like blackberries. There's no reason anyone should have to suffer."

She nodded to herself a little. "Okay. Okay, let's do it."

Searching in the back, I found an old pair of sweatpants and a pair of clean panties for her. They were a little big on her, being that they were sized for me, but they worked better than her scrubs. She still held the blanket tightly around her shoulders as I mixed up some of my elixir in a bottle. I handed her the bottle when the color changed from milky white to dark purple.

"Sip this. Don't gulp. Sipping will give you a long, easy buzz. Gulp it down and you will pass out for a long time. While that might sound appealing right now, I need you conscious."

She nodded and accepted the bottle. It only took a few sips for her lips to turn purple and her shoulders to relax. Her eyes softened and much of the fear left them.

I went about my business, preparing the lights I needed, the ink cartridges, and the laser pen. Never before had I attempted anything nearly this big. My jobs were mainly for erasing the painful things and seamlessly weaving in something more tangible. This was creating a new life from scratch. Where on earth would I begin?

She positioned herself on my chair, which was an old massage chair I had bought off of a corporate massage group that had gone tits up about five years ago. The girl rested her front against the cushions and positioned her face in the head cradle. I fired up the laser pen and loaded the ink cartridge like a bullet in a gun.

My hand hesitated over her perfectly smooth skull. The Maker had given us a break in one major respect. Our childhood was etched on our skulls. That's where it began. The beginning of your life began right about where your hairline would be and continued down from there. Therefore, most of your embarrassing childhood traumas could easily be covered up later in life by your hair. With me, very little was embarrassing, so I buzzed my hair short on the sides with coif of raven hair on the top. This let the whole world see that I had fallen in love with Tommy Singleton behind school the day he gave me a vintage T-shirt and a dried-up rose.

But this girl, what would I write? For that matter, where would her hairline start? I felt her head delicately for some sign of stubble and found none. At last, I discovered the tiniest indention in her skin where a hairline should go and kept my finger on it to mark my place.

"What would you like your birthday to be?"

She was silent for a while. "Sometime when it's warm."

That's how I began. I had seen babies, and I knew how all of our stories started. The wording was always the same, more or less. I did a quick calculation in my head and wrote the words just below her newly found hairline.

This child of mine in all her divinity was born on June Ninth, 2033.

When the sentence was finished, I stopped my pen.

"Did that hurt at all?"

"No."

"Good. Do you know when you were born?"

"June ninth, 2033," she said with wonder in her voice. "I have a birthday. Thank you."

I smiled. This might just work after all. "What would you like your name to be?"

The girl paused, unsure what to say. "Jane? Jane sounds nice, doesn't it? That's what they called me at the hospital. Jane Doe. I don't like the Doe part, but the Jane part is nice."

"I think Jane sounds great," I said reassuringly. "What about a last name?"

She drew a blank at that.

I thought of the girl and how tiny she was, how delicate like a little bird. She was a beautiful, little bird.

"Sparrow?" I offered.

"Jane Sparrow," she repeated. "I like it, like I can fly away."

I nodded and wrote her new name across her skull.

"Jane Marie Sparrow," she said when I finished. "That's my name."

"It is now," I said.

"Yes, but after you write it, it feels like it always has been."

"That's the way it works. I will make up your history by writing it across your head, down to your neck, and it will spiral around and around part way down your shoulders. That's about where most stories get to at about your age. Some longer if they've lived more, but we are probably going to end yours right about here."

I touched a part of her back just above her shoulders blades. The now-Jane flinched a little at the unexpected feeling.

"Not my face? Words are not written there?"

"No, not yet at any rate. The face is saved for final thoughts. When you are old and gray, and you die, your last thoughts and wishes are written on your face for your loved ones to see and know. All except your forehead."

"What's written on the forehead?"

I chuckled a little. "Just keep your nose clean, and nothing will be written on your forehead."

Jane sat up suddenly and looked at me seriously. "What gets written on your forehead?"

With a little coaxing, I got her to sip some more elixir and her eyes began to soften again with the fuzzy reality of the drink.

"The forehead is reserved for when you commit one of the majors. Wrath, Gluttony, and the like. Half the lawyers downtown have Greed tattooed on their foreheads and half the whores have Lust. Like I said, keep your nose clean, and you'll be fine."

She settled her head in the face cradle, and I got back to work. It was like writing a novel or something. Ideas of a lovely life just came to me. Jane's parents were Fred and Marie Sparrow. Fred was a science teacher at a high school, and Marie worked at an ad agency. They raised their daughter in San Marcos, where she spent an ideal childhood tubing in the rivers and fishing with her dad. Her favorite Christmas present ever was the year her parents bought her the purple bicycle when she was eight. This, plus her mother's love of riding, had contributed to Jane's love of cycling.

"I can see it," Jane said after I finished writing about the bicycle. "It was so beautiful, and Mom and Dad were so proud that I could ride like I could. They never needed to help me. I had perfect balance. I can remember how the paint of the bike smelled next to the Christmas tree."

She sipped more elixir, and I pressed onward.

Her first crush and kiss was from a boy in her art class in middle school. He was terribly good, and she was not. His name was Geoffrey, and he stole her little heart by drawing a portrait of her and giving it to her as a Valentine's present. She kissed him on the cheek behind his mother's van the day his family moved him away to San Antonio.

Jane sat up after that and stared at me, tears rimming her eyes.

"Why would you make him move away?"

"Honey, it can't all be perfect. No one would believe it. Besides, nobody stays with their childhood crush. A little heartbreak is good. It teaches you some valuable lessons."

I felt like a mother imparting valuable wisdom to my little girl. She still stared at me accusingly as a tear ran down her cheek. I hugged her and wrapped the blanket over her shoulders. It was time for a break, so I brought her some ice cream. Jane liked it so much that when I started up again, I made sure to include some great memories of ice cream and orange soda to make up for the Geoffrey part.

Her high school experience was awkward and unremarkable, like most of ours were. She did well in school and really enjoyed her classes. Science was her favorite, since her father had such a love of it. He imparted so much of his wonder onto her, and she ran with it, making the honor role and winning first prize for her science fair experiment in her junior year. He was so proud of her that day. She went to her senior prom with her good friend Andrew just as friends, since Andrew was gay and too afraid to tell anyone but her yet. Jane didn't care because they had a wonderful time, and no one danced like Andrew could.

I heard her giggle a little at the memory of dancing with Andrew in her light blue gown with sequins along the side. He wore a tuxedo with a bowtie that matched her dress. Jane sipped more elixir as I continued to write her story, but we were getting to her shoulders now, and I was running out of life to write. We were quickly approaching the part I really, really didn't want to do.

Jane graduated high school with honors, and had applications out to many of the nearby colleges when...

"Jane sit up," I said seriously.

She did so and looked at me. Confusion covered her face.

"This next part will be bad. I will make it as easy as I can, but it won't be pretty."

"W-why? What are you going to do?"

"Drink some more elixir."

Jane drank without hesitation.

"We have to explain why you are here in Dallas with no one to help you. I made you a lovely life with loving parents, but if they are living, where are they? Why are you alone?"

"I don't understand."

"In order for people to accept you and your story, we have to have a reason you are here alone with no connections. I'm afraid that means your parents died."

Terror filled her eyes, and she grabbed for my shirt. "No. No! Please don't. I love them. Please don't kill them. Please!"

She was desperate and clutching me in a panic. These people, these imaginary parents I invented for her, were as real to her as anything.

"Jane, honey, I have to. We can't have anyone finding out about you or about what we've done here. It's so illegal. You will never be able to live a normal life."

"I could just pretend they are there. Send letters and pictures to nobody. I could take whole trips to visit them, to keep up appearances."

She was grasping so very frantically.

"And how long could you keep that up? What if you marry? Have kids? Honey, they aren't real. One quick scan on a computer will debunk your lie. If they are deceased, no one will ask or care to look."

"But..."

"Jane, think about it. They are only a memory right now anyway. You can never see them. They are already gone."

The defeat was there in her face. I knew I had won, but I never wanted to win this one. Reason had gotten the better of her, but she didn't like it. Jane swigged another gulp of elixir to wash down the bitter taste of what was about to happen. Before she put her face in the cradle, she looked up at me pleadingly. That face could've melted stone.

"Please, please don't make it bad. I don't want them to hurt or suffer. Please?"

"I promise."

She rested back in place, and I began. Fred and Marie Sparrow were driving back from their daughter's graduation party in the rain. The road was slick and they had both had a few glasses of champagne. As they relived the beautiful evening they had just had to one another, the car unexpectedly hydroplaned, spinning off of the road and over a bridge. Fred and Marie died on impact, without a moment of fear or pain between them. The last thoughts written on their faces were of their beloved daughter and how proud they were of her.

As soon as my pen ceased, Jane jolted up and collapsed into my arms. Jagged, jerking sobs wracked her body as she clung to me. I sobbed too. I held that little bird thing and cried with her for what seemed like an eternity. We squeezed our bodies together, and wiped tears and snot all over each other. We wailed and we mourned for two imaginary people who had never lived.

When it was over, I brought us tissues and we recovered as well as we could. Deep circles hung under Jane's eyes as she stared into space, distraught and grief stricken.

"We are almost done."

She shot a look at me. "There's more?"

"It's not bad. Just something to explain why you are here. Then we will be done."

Jane drank what was left of the elixir and positioned herself for me. I finished her story to date. After her parents' deaths, she was lost. She spent most of the money they left her surviving for a while and paying the rent on the house. When that was nearly up, she decided she needed to go somewhere completely new and start over. She used most of her money buying a Speed Train ticket to Dallas. A friend knew someone named Dakota there who could help her get settled in the right places. Which brought us to the here and now.

Sighing, I sat back from my handiwork and admired it for a moment while I rubbed ointment on her newly inked life. No one would have been able to tell the difference between the life I wrote for her and any other life the Maker would have written. It was perfect.

I brought down a few old shirts I didn't wear anymore and a sports bra that might fit her. I also gave her an old Halloween wig, for which I had paid good money, and a few headscarves that would make the wig look believable. Once dressed, she looked like any other kid you might see trying to buy some cheap jewelry off me in my store. I nodded at her. Jane would be safe now.

"So, this is when I pay you, yes? I owe you flesh. I appreciate what you've done, and I will pay you. A deal is a deal."

She looked and sounded resolute. The girl was ready to pay, but I shook my head.

"Listen kid, forget about that. Just go and live a good life for me, okay? I've got enough skin to last me a year."

Her face softened and she hugged me. I wanted to say so many things to her. All night we had spent together building her life. The darkness outside was lightening with the coming sun. I wished profound words would exit my mouth to inspire her on her next journey, but they just weren't there. I squeezed her tighter and handed her a Dakota's Jewel bag that had a few extra shirts, some more scarfs, and some money.

"That's just a little cash to help you get started. There's also an address in there to a really good halfway house run by some friends of mine. Use some of that money to take a taxi there. Don't walk. Ask for Marlene and tell her Dakota sent you. They specialize in getting kids into colleges."

"But what if I'm not smart enough for college?"

"You are."

"How do you know?"

"Because I wrote you that way."

We smiled at each other. She reached in and found the other thing I had placed in the bag for her. They were a pair of earrings from my stock. It was a set of beautiful, identical sparrows.

"What's this?"

"In memory of your parents," I said.

We hugged again, and before I started crying all over myself once more, I gently pushed her away.

"All right, get out of here before anyone sees you."

I sniffed and cleared my face on a rag. With a flash of a grateful smile, the girl, now Jane, was out of my store and out of my life. The whole place suddenly seemed so empty, but I wouldn't cry again. I locked up the store and made my way up the creaky, wooden steps to my loft apartment. First, the boots came off, then the jeans, then the shirt and leather vest. I pulled on the biggest nightshirt I could find and reveled in its comfort.

The past evening had been a whirlwind, and now, I could reflect. I had created an entire life. Well, not a whole one, but one up until the cusp of adulthood. Everything I wrote was true to that girl. I had saved her. I had given her life; even though I knew the thought was wrong, I couldn't help but wonder if this was what the Maker felt. I altered memories in the past, sure I had. Sometimes, I even invented a few things here and there, but tonight, I had acted as that girl's Maker.

A crazy thought occurred to me. Would the Maker pick up where I had left off with her? Would Jane wake up tomorrow with our night together written below my writing? If that was the case, I could always erase it like I did for so many others to protect us. I knew it would probably show up on my back, but I didn't mind. The mayor made sure the cops didn't read my body.

But what if the Maker never wrote anything more for her ever again? What if whatever afflicted her plagued her further, and no writing continued at all? If that happened, I knew what I'd do. I'd do the Maker's job for Jane. I'd continue writing down her life no matter what. I'd protect that little girl. After all, in a way, I was her Maker. I wouldn't let her down.

I walked over to the sink to wash my face and brush my teeth. The time for mascara removal was long overdue. It wasn't until I looked up into the mirror that I saw it. The word was written boldly and straight across my forehead so no one could miss it. My mouth fell open, and I almost said the word aloud.

Pride

"Well, shit."

I stood there gaping at my forehead for a long time. Like a moron, my next instinct was to splash water on my hand and try to rub it off. That obviously didn't help, so I stared at myself for a long while wondering what to do and how long it had been there.

After a while, I decided what the hell. I made a kissy face at the mirror and gave myself a sexy wink.

"I guess it's time to cut some bangs," I said to my reflection.

After all, when you can't do something about it, might as well own it. There were worse things in this life to be labeled.

Chapter Six: *Toby*

Nobody seemed to recognize me. I'm not complaining, mind you. It's the way of things, and something I rather preferred to be honest. People who get noticed often do when they try to be noticed. Me? I can move about the hospital like a gray ghost leaving order in my wake. Tidy ghosts are after all the best ghosts to have around.

The uniform helped with the invisibility trick. Doctors wore white. Everyone always noticed the doctors in those bright white lab coats of theirs. Nurses came next in their blue scrubs. It was a calming blue but one you looked for because she probably had your next pill or whatever you needed. Khaki scrubs were for the orderlies. They were only barely more noticeable than me, but you saw them, especially when you didn't want to. When someone came in thrashing about all violent, that's when a whole herd of khaki took charge. Everyone noticed khaki when that happened.

Custodial staff were in gray. That was me. There was this theory of mine that they put us in the blandest color imaginable to have us blend into the background so we didn't call attention to ourselves. As if we were not really important at all. We wore gray so no one made the mistake of thinking we actually mattered. Maybe that was a bitter way to think about the whole uniform thing, but you see, the gray ghost life was my choice. I wanted to be in the background. Out of the spotlight.

I got these headaches when life blew up too colorful. That was the best way I could explain it. During high school, I had top marks without trying too hard. Everyone paid attention to me then. My mom and dad were so proud, but the more I achieved, the more attention I got, and the more my head hurt. Soon, life wasn't all about the correct things; it was about the test things. I was so good at the test things, but everyone was so overwhelmingly pre-occupied with it. As if the test things somehow explained everything you were with a number. A score, a ranking could not tell anyone what you were. It only told them that you were good at playing the game of tests.

The real things were what interested me, the life things, like music. Music was definitely a life thing. The way people discussed emotions with one another without ever saying a word, like with their eyes and their hands. That was a life thing. Someone might have a hard time looking into your eyes. Another person may find it hard not to count every ceiling tile in a room to make sure there were enough. One person may hate to hug, and the reason why is a story they don't want to tell until they know you really well. That too was a life thing.

There was a day I was taking final exams during high school. It was a test thing my parents really wanted me to do, so I did it for them. My mom, she always wore her proud smile after a test. When I came home, there was a police officer waiting with news about a traffic accident and my mom and dad. It had been a collision coming back from picking up groceries to make a big dinner for me. Dad was good at cakes. He was going to bake a red velvet one for me. What happened in the car was a bad life thing, and one I missed because of the stupid test thing I was doing. They were gone, and it was my fault. All for a test thing.

Despite all of my teachers' urging, I declined the offers of college. The University of Texas offered me a full academic scholarship, but I politely declined it. The limelight was blinding, and I didn't want it anymore. What I desired was to be invisible, a gray ghost. I wanted to continue my studies of things that mattered.

My first day as a custodian at Baylor Medical Center was the first day in years I had no headache. No one noticed me. No one cared about my test scores. No one looked at me with sad walls behind their eyes because they knew what had happened to my parents. I was in the background. I was invisible. I was free to learn.

When I learned about music, the old types that no one performed anymore, was what I liked most. Musicals were amazing when it came to generating different emotions. My favorite was a song from a play called *Chicago*. A sad man sang in a wonderfully heartbreaking way that his name was Mr. Cellophane. He was in the background, and no one noticed him. It was as if he was see-through. I loved that. I wanted that. To be Mr. Cellophane was my goal.

Music became a hobby of mine. I collected digital copies of every bit of music I could find. The act of finding a piece of music I never heard before was like finding a treasure buried beneath the sand. If music could transform my mind, perhaps it could transform others. Maybe it could change the sick people in my hospital.

The patients at Baylor became my research subjects. I collected several cheap music players capable of playing a song remotely controlled by my own handheld mixer. When no one noticed me, I would slip into someone's room with the player. My cover was that I was emptying their trashcan or sweeping the floor, but what I was really doing was planting one of my players under their bed.

When no one was about, I would play a piece of music I thought might cheer the person on that bed. It was a lot of trial and error. Apparently, not all people reacted the same to musicals as I did.

Mr. Gunterson in 213B hopped up from his bed when I played something from *Cabaret* and shouted angrily. "Where's that queer music coming from?"

It turned out, after many tries, that Mr. Gunterson really enjoyed old-style heavy metal.

Mrs. Parson down the hall from him loved the musicals I played for her, but preferred the happier songs. Mr. Terre liked the musicals all right, but hated *Grease*. Mrs. Smith detested anything that wasn't punk rock, and Mr. Turner wanted R&B. The patients on the younger floors all enjoyed the fun musicals with the silly songs, but liked the newer retro techno rap best of all.

I took diligent notes, and stocked up on players, thinking that eventually someone would report the music and my equipment would be found. The most amazing part of this experiment was that no one talked about the sudden appearance of the music. No one told their nurse about it. Even when Mr. Parks sat up and yelled that he hated fucking Barbara Streisand, no one paid him any mind at all, and he didn't report it. A wobbly theory of why was formulating in my mind that had a lot of unanswered questions in it. Real questions and not test questions, so they weren't as clear.

The day *she* appeared seemed like any other day at first. No one noticed me walk in the door. I waved hello without much eye contact to several of the nurses I recognized. A few waved back with a smile then instantly looked away from me. It wasn't until I got to the fourth floor that I noticed the difference.

It was like when you were a kid and you kicked over an anthill. The ants on the bottom of the hill didn't know anything was amiss at first, but the ones on the top levels scurried around like maniacs. Doctors, nurses and orderlies were walking hurriedly about the floor. It was never wise to be seen running in the hospital. Someone might think there was an emergency then panic. Regardless, something sure was happening, because the activity around me was deafening. The people who weren't buzzing back and forth were talking excitedly to one another. The world seemed to vibrate from tension. I didn't like it. There were too many people near me.

Excitement in a hospital was like an open wound. All the people fluttered about like white blood cells, trying desperately to know what was happening and adjust. To find the source, to find the wound, you just had to go where there was the greatest concentration of white blood cells. I followed the chaos and found a cluster of them hovering around room 462.

Some medical students milled past me, bumping into me as they went. They registered my presence long enough to mutter a quick apology before going on their way. I was not a fan of touching people in close quarters, but I shrugged it off to better hear what they were saying.

"You ever seen anything like that?"

"No. It's crazy."

"Totally unmarked. Not a tattoo on her."

"What does Dr. Patel think?"

"I don't know. I don't think she's seen her yet."

As if summoned by some Goddess of Coincidence, Dr. Patel rounded the corner, parting the milling masses in her wake. She was a pretty woman with her almond eyes and dark hair pulled back in a tight knot. Dr. Patel knew she was pretty, but she was stern and no nonsense as much as she was pretty, perhaps more so to compensate. She was intimidating even to other doctors. I backed into a corner to better disappear as she approached.

"Surely all of you have something like work to be doing," she said loud enough to disperse the crowd.

I lingered long enough to peek inside the room as the doctor entered. There, sleeping in the bed, was a perfectly unmarked girl, not one tattoo was etched on her that I could see. She was thin and fair. The door slammed in my face before I could get another look, but I knew I had to find out more.

The rumor mill around the hospital was in full force. Much of it was speculation. The bed had been empty the night before, and the morning had magically brought with her an unconscious girl. A few people had seen the girl's bald head and dubbed her an alien. Others had decided she was a military hostage being kept under wraps. The facts were she seemed to appear from nowhere, there wasn't a mark on her, and she hadn't woken yet.

Speculation was not enough to satisfy me. Seeing the girl again became my main goal. I was working a double that day, which meant I would be around at night when most people were gone. Timing would be everything. The evening would have to be planned out according to my notes on the nurses. At around nine at night, the two graveyard shift nurses ate their dinner together in the break room. It was a space that allowed them access to the callboard but no visual access to room 462. There would be a small window then to make my move.

The door to the room was locked. This was not a surprise and not a problem. Every custodian had a card key that opened every door in Baylor, a skeleton key they called it. I never knew why. At any rate, the gray ghost opened the door with the skeleton key and entered.

The girl was still unconscious. They had put an IV in her arm, but she slept just as gently as she had that morning, unaware of the scandal her presence was causing. She looked remarkable. Skin so pale and delicate and completely unmarked by any tattoo. I had thought people were pretty before. I had decided things, like music and art, were beautiful. However, I had never labeled a person beautiful before, but that's what she was. Her beauty was a real thing.

Gingerly and without a sound, I placed the remote music player underneath her bed. There was this little shelf inside the mechanical contraption that made the bed move. It was a perfect hiding spot for a player, and it was difficult to easily see unless you bent over looking for it. I had just enough time to stand back up after placing my equipment when the door to her room flew open and a nurse walked into the room. She and I met eyes, startling each other.

"Toby! What...what are you doing in here?"

Nancy was one of the only nurses who knew my name. She knew everyone and was nice to them all. That's just the kind of person she was.

"I'm cleaning the floor."

I was never good at lying, so my answer sounded hollow, as if it was full of air instead of true things. Not only that, but my mop cart was still sitting outside of the room. My eyes quivered with the knowledge of my bad lie. Her face screwed into a strange smile. It was a smile that meant she didn't believe me.

"Curious, huh?"

"Yes, Ma'am."

"I can't fault your curiosity, Toby. Everyone is curious about this one."

Together, we looked at the unconscious girl.

"Poor thing. She has no idea the world of trouble she's going to wake up to. If she ever wakes up."

"Is she okay?"

"All the tests say she's fine. We have no idea where she came from, though. I guess we'll see what she has to say. Come on, let's get out of here."

She ushered me out, being sure not to touch my shoulder like she would many of the others. Nancy was nice and knew I wouldn't like that.

With the blinds drawn and the door locked, I couldn't test different music on the girl and accurately record her reactions. There would be no way to watch for visual cues. The video feed of her room went straight to the nurses' station, and someone was there all the time. My only alternative was to choose music for her and hope she liked it.

This was a frustrating dilemma. I didn't know anything about the girl. Often, a person's age clued me in to their preferences, but the younger music seemed too rambunctious for her for some reason. The old musicals I liked didn't feel right either. When I came to a conclusion, it was one that seemed obvious retrospectively. She was beautiful without words, and the most beautiful music I could think of without words was classical music. The most fitting classical pieces I knew for a girl like her were Chopin's Nocturnes. They told so much without ever saying a thing. Just listening to them reminded me of her.

I pressed play on my mixer and waited. While I sat in the shadows of the empty room down the hall, I imagined the girl hearing the lovely music without words and it rousing her from her sleep. Her eyes would flutter open to the perfection of the human soul. I pictured her first memory of this new waking world to be Chopin, and I really hoped she wasn't a techno fan.

After a few minutes, there was a commotion at the nurses' station. Emma, the other nurse on duty, was running toward room 462 all wide-eyed and calling for Nancy. Excitement coursed through my body, and I was so giddy I almost forgot to press the stop button on my mixer before the two nurses raced inside the room.

As silently as I could manage, I followed behind them and peered into the open door. It was opened just enough for me to have a little vertical window. There, sitting straight up and smiling, was the girl. She was awake. The nurses busied themselves around her, asking her questions and the like. Her big, brown eyes drank them in as she looked around, a sense of wonder in her face as if the world was a new and terribly grand place to be.

Then, she met my eyes. I stood awkwardly in the doorway, not knowing what to do. Without hesitation, she smiled at me and waved as if we had been friends a long time. I smiled too and waved back, even as Nancy excused me and shut the door in between us. It didn't matter all that much. I had learned enough for one night.

The beautiful girl loved Chopin.

The next day, everyone whispered. Yesterday, the rumors had been practically shouted around the hospital. People galloped like herds of African beasts and huddled around her room. Now that she was awake, the din became a whisper. The persistent yammering continued, but she could hear it now. For some reason, that fact made everyone tiptoe. Strange rumors began to abound, but the one consistent one was the girl had no memory whatsoever.

For the first time, I had a legitimate excuse to enter the girl's room. Her waste basket needed emptying and the floor needed a good mop. I entered the room like a gray ghost, trying to blend into the background. As soon as the door shut behind me, I looked up to see the girl staring directly into my eyes with a large grin, just as she had the night before. In any other situation, I might have looked away. It wasn't often that someone looked directly at me in that manner, and when it did happen, I usually became instantly uncomfortable. The little twinge in the pit of my stomach would flare into my chest, and the eye contact would be too much for me to bear.

That didn't happen this time though. No twinges and no fluttering in my chest. Even her room smelled different. Most had the scent of antiseptic and sometimes body smells like urine or worse. Many people went nose blind to these sorts of things about a hospital, but I never seemed to. The beautiful girl's room smelled like incense or burnt flowers, as if someone mixed sandalwood and jasmine together in a bowl and slowly burned the best parts of it into the air.

"Hello," she said to me. "What's your name?"

I looked into her eyes, all big and round like a deer.

"I'm Toby."

"I don't know my name. Everyone keeps asking, but I don't know what to tell them. Do you know what my name is?"

I shook my head, and she looked disappointed for a second.

It was eerie every time I looked at her after looking somewhere else. The lack of tattoos was always startling at first, but as soon as my eyes adjusted, all I saw was how lovely and fragile she was.

In a whirl of motion, Dr. Patel burst into the door with tests results and other papers in her hands. I quickly got back to my duties, breaking eye contact with the girl. Dr. Patel didn't seem to see me at all. Once again I was the gray ghost.

"Hello, I'm Dr. Patel."

"Hello, Dr. Patel."

"It says here that you don't remember who you are."

"Yes, that's right."

I looked over at the pretty doctor. She was still in that initial state of fright after seeing the girl. The jarring notion of what she was that didn't seem right. It was like looking at someone who had been badly burned or scarred. The different nature of their appearance shocked your system, but eventually your brain told you they were alive, human, and deserving of your respect. Dr. Patel's eyes seemed to stay in that state of fear while she studied the girl. Her voice was stern and clinical in its tone, but under her eyes, the good doctor was screaming.

"Well, all of your tests came back clean. You are perfectly healthy."

"That's good."

Dr. Patel was staring down at her papers and seemed suddenly focused on what was written there. I knew better; it was a trick the other doctors had when they had bad news and didn't want to face the patient. While I didn't think Dr. Patel had bad news just then, I did believe she was using this trick to not look at the girl any longer than necessary.

"Yes, it is. I will assign a psych evaluator to come in and have a talk with you."

"Thank you."

The doctor nodded and left the room without another word, still staring intently at the papers before her, as though to reveal some mystery.

A slimy thing moved in my stomach and threatened to expel my breakfast. If Dr. Patel, a woman who had seen and treated all manner of horrific wounds and diseases, flinched in fear at the girl's appearance, what would a regular person do? What would an evil person do?

I hurriedly finished up what I was doing, and when I packed up my mop cart and turned around, the girl was staring at me again, eyes wide and honest. Looking into those eyes, a person could get lost. I wasn't used to that. I never wanted to get lost while sharing glances with others, but for whatever reason, this was all right.

"I know why," she said out of nowhere.

"You know why what?"

"Why they don't report you. About the music, I mean. I know why none of the patients report the music you play."

My breath caught. How had she known? I only played music to her the one night. My mouth went dry, so I licked my lips. It didn't seem to help.

"Why?"

"Because it makes them feel real."

"Real?"

"Yes, the music makes you feel alive. In here, you feel like a thing. Something they are keeping alive, something they poke and test. The music reminds them they are people, they are real. They don't want to risk losing it."

I stood there just looking at her. My mouth might have been slack. It was hard to tell. With a nod, I left her room a different man. In five minutes, the girl had turned my entire world upside down. Then, I thought about Dr. Patel and her horrible expression, the horror she was hiding and what that might make her do. I looked across the brightly lit hall of level four to see the good doctor talking in fierce whispers with two of her other colleagues. Dark clouds threatened the corners of my eyes.

I must have been standing there a while because it took Nancy several tries to get my attention.

"Toby? Hey kid, you okay?"

When I had snapped out of it, I looked down at the small nurse. I had a good six inches on her. "Nancy, we need to get her out of here."

"What do you mean?"

"I think something bad is going to happen."

"You off your meds, kid? We can't just cut her loose."

"I don't take meds."

Nancy looked ashamed for a second then continued, "Sorry, Toby. I didn't mean that, but we can't just bust her out of the hospital based on some hunch you've got."

I pointed at the gathering of doctors in the corner. Nancy followed my gaze. She was a practical woman, but she was also smart. The sweet nurse picked up on the real things in life just like I did, and the danger in that gathering was open for anyone to see. Her back visibly tensed.

"What's going on?" she asked.

"Have you seen the doctors look at the girl?"

"Yeah."

"But not for long."

"Toby, just because they are uncomfortable doesn't mean something bad is going to happen."

I looked down at her again. The area behind my eyes began to get hot.

"Look, before you do anything drastic, let me do some snooping. I'll find out what's going on. Just trust me a little, okay?"

"Okay."

"Now, get back to work before anyone sees you spying."

The day passed slowly. I never was one to watch the clock. Things like that were ridiculous pastimes for those who didn't have experiments and real things to accomplish. However, despite all my best efforts, I found myself watching the clock all day, waiting for it to tick down. I did my work, but it didn't occupy me. My mind was in room 462, with the beautiful girl. Waiting was a terrible thing. It felt like living in the middle of a fall. You were no longer where you started, but you had not yet hit the ground. Floating was a good word for it, but it didn't hold enough meaning. Regardless, the day was an agony.

The clock had nearly struck seven when Nancy found me out back emptying the dirty water of my mop cart behind the dumpster. Her eyes were wild and frightened, and I immediately pushed the sweetly putrid scent of garbage out of my nose to pay her my full attention. The woman's small frame twitched as if she was being zapped again and again.

"You're right. We need to get her out."

"You heard something."

"No. Well...yes. I don't want to say what I heard. Just listen to me. We need to get her out of this hospital tonight."

"She can come stay with me," I offered.

"No she can't. This is bigger than us, Toby. She needs to be with people who can start her on a new life. People who can help her hide. I'm going to give her the information for a tattooist friend of mine."

"You know a tattooist?"

The shock in my voice was sincere. I knew of such people, but had never met one. Perhaps I had and didn't know it. At any rate, the idea of covering the beautiful girl in tattoos seemed wrong somehow.

"Yes, and that's the last I want to say on the matter. She has no other good alternative. We need to get her out of here and get her marked."

I wholeheartedly agreed with the first part even if I didn't agree with the last. For hours I had been wracking my brain for an answer to her problem, and nothing better than this had come to me. Pondering Nancy's tattooist friend would be something I did another time.

"What do you need me to do?"

"Go to lost and found and scrounge up some clothes that might fit her. Hoodies and pants are the best. The more of her skin we can hide the better. Come up to level four at nine. Logan is on duty with me, but he always goes for a break at nine to call his girlfriend. It's like clockwork. When he does, I will shut off the cameras to the whole floor and say there was a glitch and I had to reboot the system. While the cameras are down, we will get her in a cab."

"Have you...done this before?"

"Shut up and do what I say."

"Yes, Ma'am."

Before I could do anything else besides stare at her in amazement, Nancy shoved her hands into the pockets of her blue scrubs and ran back inside.

I did as instructed. On level one stood the lost and found locker. Children's toys, old scrubs with tire marks on them, and an ancient camera that didn't work. These were the contents of the locker. I managed to find a worn-out hoodie and a pair of scrub pants that weren't too banged up. Both would probably bag on the girl, but they'd do. No underwear and no bras. Mostly, that stuff got thrown in the garbage. I wouldn't know what size to get her anyway.

Me and my mop cart arrived on level four five minutes before nine. The place was a ghost town. Visiting hours ended at eight and each level only staffed a bare skeleton crew at night. Nancy made eye contact with me from the nurses' station. Logan was already on his phone and heading to the elevator. He nodded as we passed each other.

As soon as the elevator door closed, Nancy threw the power switch for the level four room cameras. We raced into room 462 in perfect synchronicity.

The beautiful girl looked up in surprise as we did. "What's going on?"

"We are getting you out of here," said Nancy as she quickly shut off the machines around the girl's bed.

Various wires and tubes had to be disconnected before the girl was free. A soft-sounding alarm went off, but Nancy promptly silenced it. I handed her the bundle of clothes and turned away to give her and Nancy some privacy while she helped the girl get dressed. When they were done, she almost looked normal. Her bald head was concealed under the hood of her jacket.

"Take this. You will give it to the driver of the car Toby will put you into. The name of the woman you need to see is Dakota. She is at this address. Dakota will help you."

"Why?"

For a minute, we weren't sure which why this was. Did she mean why would Dakota help her or why was she leaving? Both questions were equally important.

"Because if you stay here, something bad will happen to you," said Nancy.

The girl's face turned serious, perhaps for the first time since she had woken. She looked afraid, and I was sorry to see her that way.

"Don't worry. We are here to help you," explained Nancy. "Me and Toby. We are trying to get you to a safe place. Toby, do you have any cash on you?"

I thought for a second about the contents of my wallet.

"I have exactly forty-seven dollars."

"Okay, I have twenty. Hand it over, Toby. That will get you to Deep Ellum and get you some food. Dakota will help with the rest. She has more connections than I do."

We combined the money, and Nancy stuffed it into the girl's hoodie pockets. It wasn't until we left her room that we heard the all too familiar voice of Logan at the nurses' station.

"Hey. Why the hell are all the cameras down?"

I was just about the step out into the open hallway when a tiny, white hand grabbed my large, brown one and yanked me back inside the safety of the room. Looking down, I saw the hand was the girl's. It felt warm and soft in mine. Normally, I hated touching other people. Holding hands was rarely an activity I enjoyed. But this? This was nice.

Nancy hurried out of the room in a mock flurry.

"The damn cameras are off all over the floor. I don't know what happened. Can you check the main power box in the storage closet?"

Logan agreed and walked purposefully away from us toward the storage closet on the other side of the floor. Nancy turned to the darkness in room 462, where we were hiding, and motioned for us to make a run for it. At that point, I was thoroughly convinced she had done this before.

With me still holding the girl's tiny hand, we raced across the floor to the elevator. Trying to run silently was a struggle. Thankfully, Nancy planned a sneezing fit right as we began our mad dash. The two of us exhaled a mutually held breath when the door opened as if it had been waiting for us. Ducking inside the elevator, I noticed I had forgotten one key piece of clothing. The girl was barefoot.

"Here," I said unlacing my sneakers. "You can have mine."

I had my shoes off and tied onto her feet before the elevator had opened to the ground floor. When I stood back up, she was smiling at me again, but there was no time to revel in it. I took her hand and led her through the empty lobby and out into the receiving area where the taxis stood vigilant in the evening air. The first cab we saw had a disinterested driver standing beside it. Without a second glance, he got into his taxi and nodded when the girl handed him the address.

My heart was thudding feverishly. It was all like a movie. Any moment someone would come bursting out of the door to Baylor, screaming for us to get back inside. Perhaps they'd have a gun and threaten to shoot me. I imagined they'd call me a thief, and I'd kiss the girl goodbye right before the taxi sped off with her safely inside. I'd seen enough movies like that to make it feel like a possibility.

None of that happened. No one chased us, because this wasn't a movie. Instead, I observed her in front of the opened door to the taxicab, wishing I had words for her that were real. Perfect words. Authentic words. I didn't have them. The words in my head were test words, not the real ones. They were the words you were taught to say, and those were never enough.

The girl touched my face. It was a gesture that made me slow down and really look at her with a clear mind.

"Thank you so much, Toby."

Then the beautiful girl threw her arms around me and hugged my neck. If holding hands was something I rarely liked, hugging was something I *never* allowed. It always made me feel trapped and scared, as if there was nowhere I could go from there. But hugging the girl was different. It felt warm. I could smell the flowery scent that had permeated room 462, and when I hugged her back, I didn't feel trapped at all. I felt whole and all enveloping. Words came to me. Terrified words, loving words, words that made no sense at all. Words like "forever" and "always."

"Please be safe," was all that I could say into the crook of her neck.

Never before had I meant so much in each one of those little words. Each letter held more meaning than it was ever meant to.

The driver honked, separating us from our reverie. Within seconds, the girl was in the taxi and driving away from Baylor hospital, away from me. I could still feel the warmth of her on my clothes. That odd scent of her soaked into my gray ghost scrubs. I watched the taxi drive her away while I stood in the parking lot in my worn socks. The uncomfortably hot sensation of the asphalt seeped up through my socks, reminding me where my shoes were.

There was nothing left for me to do, so I just kept repeating those words over and over again like a mantra or a spell. Every syllable had as much real stuff, as much meaning, as I could manage.

"Please be safe. Please be safe. Please be safe."

The gray ghost was finally alive.

Chapter Seven: *They*

———◦———

We entered the empty hospital room the way we usually entered rooms. One moment we were not there, and the next, the very air molecules in the space vibrated us into being. We no more walked into a room or opened a door as any enlightened being might. One simply had no need for such physical expenditure, not when you transcended physicality altogether.

She insisted on a disguise even though I had changed the air to suit our need for privacy. Humans might have walked by the empty the room, they might even wanted to go inside and see why the blinds were drawn, but they wouldn't. The air told them not to. The air said to go away and forget this room existed for now.

Still, she knew I would humor her, and both of us appeared disguised in doctor scrubs with white lab coats. Her beautiful red locks were tied up in a mound on her head, and my scars peeking their gnarled heads above the collar of my coat. Both of us looked down at the empty hospital bed before us. It was the natural state of Gods to look down on things.

"Did you bring it?" she asked me.

"Of course."

With flick of the finger, I brought forth a clay sculpture of a lovely young woman. She was gentle-looking and frail, beautiful and timid. One minute the bed before us was empty, another minute, there she was. A lovely statue in repose. A bit of art to be proud of.

"I assumed we would be calling *it* a *she* by now," I said with a tender affection as I gazed down at my creation.

"Not until I've had my say," she replied, leaning down to the motionless creature.

She touched the clay girl's delicate features lightly with one finger, tracing the fragile lines of her arms, shoulders, and face. It gave me bumps all over my burnt flesh to watch her touch my sculpture that way. It was as if she were touching me instead.

"She really is beautiful. Your best yet," she mused.

With a gentle movement, she leaned down to be face to face with the girl. A sudden clench of fear hit me, and I stopped her.

"Is this wise?" I asked her with one hand on her shoulder.

"Dear love, don't let fear weaken your resolve. Fear is such an ugly thing, don't you think? Useless really. Honestly, you used to be so brazen."

I removed my hand and stepped back.

Without a second's hesitation, she leaned back down to the clay girl. Their lips almost touched. She took in a deep inhalation of life-giving air, making sure to filter out the negative bits, and kissed the clay girl beneath her. Her lungs blew all of its contents into the lips of the sculpture, filling her up with life.

The girl's clay skin softened into flesh, her chest and belly rose with her first inhalation, and she marked the moment of her birth by uttering a sigh. When it was all over, the clay girl was no longer clay but all girl. Her flawless flesh became as pale as porcelain, yet soft and malleable. The baldness of her head stayed that way, but the eyebrows on her face took on the color of a mousey brown. Both of us looked down upon our creation with pleasure.

"Now, it is a she," she said with a triumphant smile.

"She seems so fragile. Are you sure it was wise to make her so?" I asked while covering the girl with a nearby blanket.

Now that she was alive, it seemed only right to treat her with a modicum of decency and care. She twitched a little at the sensation of a blanket touching her new skin but remained asleep all the same.

"I think it's perfect. She will attract the good kind of followers."

I nodded imperceptibly. Being so fragile, the girl would attract kindness. Even the color of her pale skin was a done with a purpose. Porcelain and egg shells, these were fair things that broke easily. They were things to be held gently. Precious treasures to be treated with kindness and love. Of course, it was her skin that would cause fear as well. That thought made me shudder and feel that old, familiar anxiety.

"When did you tell him to get here?" I asked.

"I'm already here," he said in a deep voice.

A brown-skinned being appeared behind us. His face was fierce and had the molded snout of a ram. Likewise, his dark cords of hair curled into a spiraled pattern around his cheek bones. He was not in disguise; thus, he was bare-chested and skirted in gold and blue. Somehow, despite the animalistic quality of his features, he still seemed handsome in a way only the Egyptian Gods could manage.

She acted startled in a flirting way as she turned to our comrade. Best to make him think he frightened her a little. Playing to a man's ego was second nature when it got you what you wanted. I chose to not play along, crossing my arms over my chest with a scowl. Old grudges died hard, even among Gods.

"Khnum, how good of you to come," she crooned.

"Athena," he said by way of greeting with a smile.

"How I do love the old names. Don't you?" she asked. "As if we are still the same beings in the books they read."

"Indeed, but I do not understand this gown you are wearing," Khnum said with his hands on her hips as he viewed her in full. "It is not flattering. No offense intended of course. I just prefer you as I used to know you, in golden armor and smeared with blood."

"I see. So you were not so impressed with me when I was surrounded by books. Only when I was bloodied?" she asked, not sounding offended at all.

"I loved you then too, but it was quite something to see you in battle."

"I think you just liked my helmet," said Athena as she leaned into the flirtation with her body.

They hugged as old friends might, and then as lovers might. She wrapped one arm serpent-like up the back of spiraling ropes of hair. The Egyptian God held her waist and pulled her in closely. She tilted her head upward to meet Khnum's face. They kissed long and tenderly.

I was helpless to stop them, but I was also helpless to turn away. A form of torment that.

When the kiss ended, they released one another. Athena wore a coy smile on her lips as she untangled herself from the handsome Egyptian God. She drifted back over to me and reached for my hand. I pulled it away. Khnum took note of the gesture between us and greeted me with a smile.

"Prometheus," he said by way of a greeting.

"Khnum," I said with a snort.

Tense air choked what little good air was left. In an attempt to move forward, the Egyptian God gazed about the ordinary-looking hospital room with his painted eyes, looking for something in particular. When he saw the girl, he smiled again.

"This is her?" Khnum asked.

"Yes. Isn't she lovely?" crooned Athena.

"I haven't seen her like. Well done, Prometheus."

I made a grunting noise.

"So, I must ask, Athena. Has your father—"

"My father is enjoying his retirement far too much to care about what I am doing. The affairs of mortals are no concern to him," she said.

"I see. And the newest God, the one they've been fighting over for so long?"

"The last time I saw her, she was stomping off toward the mountain. Mumbling something like, 'if they are so fond of judging one another, I'm going to leave them to it,'" she said, laughing.

"I always thought it was a he," I retorted.

"Those omnipresent mono Gods always seem to be both. All that pressure of being omnipotent. You have to be everywhere and all things. It gets to them. Identity crisis and all that," added Khnum.

"I think she's done with the lot of them," said Athena.

"That's why I'm here, I take it?"

"Absolutely, Khnum. Did you bring it?"

"Of course I did."

Khnum took out one large hand and in it was the tiny body of human fetus sculpted in clay. Athena peered in his palm to look at the creature, so small and perfect. It looked like a sculpture of something aquatic from the depths of the sea. A tiny fish as it were with nubs where appendages might someday sprout forth. Even I had to admit it was lovely. Of course, I'd never tell Khnum as much and give him the satisfaction, but I thought it all the same.

"Are you positive you want to do this?" Khnum asked them. "When it's done, there is no going back. It took quite an effort to make this one. I'm not what I once was."

It had to have taken a great deal to make something so tender and small. My jealousy over the older God's ability electrified the very air around us even though I tried to keep it in check. Athena would never understand this rivalry with Khnum. I had made the girl, after all, and was she not lovely enough? No, it wasn't about the girl. It wasn't even about the fetus. I hated Khnum for reasons that had nothing to do with clay.

"It's perfect," I admitted with a sour taste in my mouth.

"What if this doesn't work?" asked Khnum.

"It will. It did before," she said.

"All right," said Khnum handing the tiny sculpture over to Athena.

She cradled the miniscule fetus in her hand, and smiled down at the thing with all the love of a mother. The force of the air she breathed into it was nothing compared to what it took for the girl. It was such a small being, but the intensity of the effort behind it was staggering. That breath was concentrated with intentions and love and power. The density of it could collapse whole worlds and make a black hole from the sun.

The fetus became not clay but flesh. Though it looked like little more than a tadpole, I could hear the sudden and ever present thudding of its tender heart. She gently laid the tadpole inside the belly of the girl sleeping on the bed. There was no incision or blood. Athena merely moved her hand and its contents beneath her skin. When her hand was removed, the fetus was gone, tucked gently into the girl's abdomen.

"It's done."

Everyone breathed in relieved air. Even I smiled at the liberation of the deed being done. There was no turning back now. Khnum studied the two of us with curiosity.

"I never have understood you two and your obsession with the mortals. Why are you doing this?"

"Because their God left them," said Athena.

"We all left them at one time or another. Either the humans moved on, or we left on our own accord. What's the difference?"

"There's always been someone to take over before," I said. "The people are not doing well on their own. Things have not been balanced since their mono-God abandoned them."

"And this girl is going to fix it?"

Athena reached out and patted the girl's flat stomach as gentle as a kitten. If skin, with all its pores and flaws, could ever be called perfect, this sleeping girl's would be. It was like petting porcelain with a pulse, warm in all the ways stone was cold. Even though the tiny thing inside this womb could do little more than have a heartbeat right now, I imagined it moving toward her outstretched fingers.

"No, but he will."

About the Author

Michelle Rene is a creative advocate and the author of a number of published works of science fiction, historical fiction, humor and everything in between. You may have also seen her work under the pen names Olivia Rivard and Abigail Henry. She has won several indie awards for her historical fiction novel, I Once Knew Vincent.

Michelle's favorite places in the world are museums, galleries, and libraries. Everyone who creates tells a story of some kind or another. Whether she's painting, writing, or making a video game, Michelle is dedicated to her obsession with storytelling.

When not writing, she is a professional artist and all around odd person. She lives as the only female, writing in her little closet, with her husband, son, and ungrateful cat in Dallas, Texas.

About the Publisher

Annorlunda Books is a small press that publishes books to inform, entertain, and make you think. We publish short writing (novella length or shorter), fiction or non-fiction. Our publication criteria are simple: if we like it and it taught us something new or made us think, we'll publish it.

Find more information about us and our books online at annorlundaenterprises.com/books/, on Facebook at facebook.com/annorlundabooks/, or on Twitter at @AnnorlundaInc.

To stay up to date on all of our releases, subscribe to our mailing list at annorlundaenterprises.com/mailing-list/

Other Titles from Annorlunda Books

Original Short eBooks and Collections

The Lilies of Dawn, by Vanessa Fogg, is a fantasy novelette about love, duty, family, and one young woman's coming of age.

Water into Wine, by Joyce Chng, is a sci-fi novella about a family trying to build a life amidst an interstellar war that threatens everything.

Both Sides of My Skin, by Elizabeth Trach, is a collection of short stories exploring the reality of pregnancy and motherhood.

The Burning, by J.P. Seewald, is a novella set in the coal country of Pennsylvania, about a family struggling to cope as a slow-moving catastrophe threatens everything they have..

Unspotted, by Justin Fox, is the story of the Cape Mountain Leopard, the scientist dedicated to saving these rare and elusive big cats, and the author's own journey to try to see one.

Caresaway, by DJ Cockburn, is a near future "inside your head" thriller about a scientist who discovers a cure for depression, but finds that it comes at a terrible cost.

Okay, So Look, by Micah Edwards, is a humorous, accurate and thought-provoking, retelling of The Book of Genesis.

Don't Call It Bollywood, by Margaret E. Redlich, is an introduction to the world of Hindi film.

Navigating the Path to Industry, by M.R. Nelson, is a hiring manager's advice on how to run a successful non-academic job search.

Academaze, by Sydney Phlox, is a collection of essays and cartoons about the tenure track and beyond at a research university.

Taster Flights

Hemmed In is a collection of classic short stories about women's lives.

Love and Other Happy Endings is a collection of classic short love stories that all end on a high note.

Missed Chances is another Taster Flight of classic stories about love. In each of its five stories, there is a hint of "the one that got away."

Small and Spooky is a collection of classic ghost stories that feature a child. These stories are spooky with a hint of sweet.

CPSIA information can be obtained
at www.ICGtesting.com
Printed in the USA
BVOW09s0545260218
509068BV00001B/66/P